FACING THE PAST

A Novella of Hope and Healing

SYLVIA A. NASH

Published by Fractured Time Press.

First Edition: June 2021

Printed in the United States of America.

ISBN-13: 978-1-7350694-4-9 (Paperback)

Scripture quotations are from The Holy Bible, King James Version.

Cover Image (Fog and Mountains)
© Betty4240 / Dreamstime.com

For if ye forgive men their trespasses,
your heavenly Father will also forgive you:
But if ye forgive not men their trespasses,
neither will your Father forgive your trespasses
(Matthew 6:14-15 KJV).

ACKNOWLEDGMENTS

I am indebted to those who advised, informed, and encouraged me as I was writing *Facing the Past*. Any errors or misinterpretation of the facts are my responsibility alone.

CHAPTER ONE

Wednesday, June 9, 2021

Josephine Chandler dropped her book into her handbag and stood as Dr. Catherine Weber opened the door between her office and the waiting room.

"Jo, come on in."

"Thanks, Dr. Weber. By the way, have I ever told you how much your pleasant demeanor and ever-present smile put me at ease?"

Jo admired more than that. Dr. Weber inspired her to care not only for her mental health but for her physical health and personal appearance as well. No matter the place or time of day, Dr. Weber never failed to look impeccable. Not a strand of her short black hair out of place, her gray eyes always sparkling, her porcelain skin flawless. And a healthy weight for her height, both of which matched Jo's but which she could only maintain with a vigorous workout and self-defense schedule.

"I don't think you have. I'm glad they do, but I'm not sure about the always part. You do remember when you first came by to schedule an appointment, don't you?"

"I do. It was after your office hours, and you were painting your office walls."

"My hair was sticking out in every direction, and my baggy work jeans were spattered with both old and new paint."

They both laughed as they made themselves comfortable in the two armchairs across from each other.

"I also remember that your appearance kind of fit with what I had told one of my classmates before that first meeting."

"What was that?"

"I struggled through my first years here—in Nashville and at Vanderbilt. I thought about seeing a psychiatrist a gazillion times for a gazillion reasons, but I was afraid to. Plus, taking care of Tanner, holding down a job, and staying on top of my schoolwork took all my energy. I was afraid if I ever stopped long enough to deal with my issues, I would crash and wouldn't be able to continue. I wouldn't allow myself to even develop friendships with but two people, one older woman at work and one classmate. I never discussed anything about my past with the older woman. I did in time talk around it with my classmate. After my eye-opening experience in the creative writing class I took spring semester of my junior year, I decided it was time to deal with my issues—before I entered the workplace full time. My classmate recommended you." Jo chuckled. "She said you were both a psychiatrist and a psychotherapist. I told her that was just what I needed—a therapist who was psycho! I kept visualizing Norman Bates, and I almost didn't come even then!"

"You never told me that either."

"I didn't dare!" Jo rolled her eyes in mock fear.

"But you came."

"I did. I was pretty messed up when we began. I'm still messed up, but at least I've made progress."

"You have made a great deal of progress. Anything of note since our last visit?"

Jo spent the next half hour updating Dr. Weber on recent events since graduation and going to work full time at the hospital.

"This is all good," said Dr. Weber.

"Yes, it is. With your help, I've managed to turn all that hurt and anger that threatened to destroy me into the driving force that carried me through school, work, and those first years of motherhood." Jo wrung her hands and looked out the window. "Nevertheless…."

"Nevertheless…?"

Jo squirmed as she turned back to face Dr. Weber. "You periodically remind me that someday I'm going to need—

maybe want—to literally face the past and those in it. You're probably right. You usually are. And I've thought about it. I've even thought about the possibility that I wasn't his only victim, that by not telling, I was responsible for any victims after me."

"Jo, your voice might have warned others and prevented his actions if you had been believed, but you are not responsible for anything he might have done."

"I know that in my head. Maybe not in my heart. Even so, I wasn't convinced the truth always sets us free. So many people would have been hurt if I had told the truth six years ago. And then the stress of 2020—trying to care for my son, finish my program, work at the hospital even part time, and resort to online appointments in the middle of a pandemic—forced me to push away thoughts of home and the past. I still don't want to think about them. I want to pretend none of it ever happened. I want to live in the present—and only in the present. But...." Jo took a deep breath.

"But...?"

"But the shadows are in every corner." Jo compressed her body as if she wanted to shrink into herself. "I can't banish them, and I'm afraid I'll stay frozen in time and space if I don't. In some ways, that doesn't bother me. But in one way, it bothers me very much. I can't let go enough to move forward with Noah. I want to, but I can't. How can I expect him to face my past if I can't face it myself? How can I have a future with him if I can't tell him about Tanner's father, my parents, the PCOS?"

"So you care about Noah Benton, and you want your relationship to progress."

"I do care about him," said Jo as she sat back and opened her arms toward Dr. Weber, "and I do want our relationship to progress, but I can't let him in. I can't get close to him or let him get close to me—emotionally or physically. He's been so patient, but that can't last forever."

"Does he want a relationship? With you? With Tanner?"

"Yes, he does. He doesn't push it, but he doesn't shy away from it either. He says he's ready when I'm ready. As for Tanner, Noah loves him. And Tanner loves Noah." Jo chuckled. "Tanner is always asking Noah to spend the night with him. He says his bed is big enough for both of them."

"Noah is a good man. I'm sure you know that. Are you afraid your issues will be a problem for him? Or is there something about him that's holding you back?"

"No, no. It's not about him at all. It's about me. I cannot build a relationship on lies, and I cannot tell him the truth. Not yet. I don't think my issues would be a problem for him, at least maybe not the polycystic ovary syndrome. He is a doctor after all. But Tanner's father? My parents? I can't be sure. If they were problematic for him, I'm afraid that would undo all the progress I have made."

"Have you told him anything?"

"Nothing."

"Has he asked?"

"No. Not outright. But he hints. And at some point, I know he will ask. What do I do then? If I can't tell *him* the truth, how can I ever face the past—or those who still wait there?"

"And he's never asked questions about Tanner?"

"No, but I've never volunteered anything either that might have given him an opportunity to ask more. Not about Tanner. Not about anything. At the beginning, when we were getting to know each other on a friend level, he would ask things like where I was from and what I was like as a child."

"And what did you tell him?"

"Nothing. I'd say, 'I don't talk about the past,' and I'd change the subject. He never insisted I say more, and eventually he stopped asking."

"Has he told you about himself and his childhood?"

"Oh, yes. Truth is, as he saw me come out of your office one afternoon shortly after we met, I'm sure he figures I have an issue of some kind, and as I don't talk about my childhood or youth, he no doubt suspects something traumatic happened then. We spoke to each other that day, but neither of us has ever mentioned it since then or the reason I might have been here. I'm guessing he thinks if he's patient long enough, I'll tell him what it was. I'm beginning to think I'll never be able to do that, though."

"I'm glad you shared this. I know you've made progress, and you're more self-assured now than you were three years ago. But have you not shared any of this with anyone other than me?"

"Only with Paige."

"Do you think your relationship with and your reliance on Paige traps you in the past? Prevents you from breaking its hold on you?"

"Could be. I never thought about it. But I could never let her go. We love each other. She was always more of a sister to me than my sister was. I would not have made it through that first year after I left home if it had not been for her support even at a distance."

"And we're both thankful for that. I'm not suggesting you sever your relationship with her at all. I'm only concerned that she might also be what binds you to the hurt and even prevents you from facing it. Jo, do you want a reconciliation with your parents?"

Jo frowned and tapped the arms of her chair with closed fists. "Not really. I don't want to cause Tanner any grief."

"If you ever do want to reconcile, you don't want to wait until it's too late."

"You mean until after my parents—or Tanner's father—passes? Then I wouldn't have to worry about it, would I?"

"Not necessarily. Then you might worry about it more. You might even grieve that as much as you grieve their passing."

"I would grieve my parents passing but not the passing of Tanner's father."

"But you have no desire to see your parents now."

"No. Well, I guess on some level, I do. If we could be like we were when I was a little girl. But I know seeing them again would require telling them what happened six years ago. There would be no way around it. And I don't want to traumatize or scar Tanner with the details of what happened."

"We've talked at length about what happened during your late teens, but we haven't yet discussed your earlier years. Do you feel any of your troubles began earlier than your teens?"

"Hmm." Jo frowned and stared out the window. "Some of it may have begun earlier." She looked at her watch. "But my time is almost up."

Dr. Weber checked her own watch. "It is, isn't it? How about we take this up next time?"

"That might be a good idea."

"In the meantime, think on this. Sometimes you have to visit the past in order to have peace in the present."

"Now that's a good quote for a pillow."

"Yes, it is."

They both smiled, and Jo stood to leave.

** * **

As Jo left Dr. Weber's office, she bit her lip in thought. *When did it begin? When I entered my teens?*

She did a mental time warp and visualized her gangly thirteen-year-old self with only a hint of the womanly contours that would grace her five-foot four-inch adult frame.

Even then she had the same straight golden-brown hair, although she wore it longer, sometimes halfway down her back. She fingered the tresses that now barely reached her shoulders. Her amber eyes were lighter then than now, but her tan was darker. Then she ran every day and played outside as much as she could. She still ran and worked out, but now she did so for her health and not so much for the joy of running.

Thirteen, she thought. *That is when everything flip-flopped inside, outside, and around me.*

At thirteen, she was a happy, loving, bubbly, full-of-life child one day and a brooding, angry, depressed in-between she didn't know the next. That's when her mom said it began. Her dad said she had always had a stubborn, rebellious streak. She had, and it was one he could trigger with a word or a look. She never knew whether he did so intentionally or not when she was younger. She was certain he did when she got older. It was like a tug-of-war between them.

Thirteen was also when the looks, the touching, and the insinuations began. She never spoke to her dad or her mom about them. She wished she had. But at the time, she didn't think they would believe her. She wasn't certain she believed it herself. She had convinced herself that either she was misinterpreting what was happening, or she was doing something to encourage it. But she had no idea what she was doing wrong. Either scenario stressed her already stressed hormones and teenage angst until she made certain she was never in a room alone with anyone other than her parents and her sister. Even that couldn't protect her from the looks. In the end, she couldn't protect herself at all.

If thirteen was when everything flip-flopped, eighteen was when everything turned upside down. She was twenty-four now, but sometimes she still felt like a vulnerable child.

She blinked at the blinding light as she left the medical building and headed for the parking garage. In contrast to her dark thoughts, the bright sun lifted her spirits. She loved summer. As a child, it meant sunlight and a world filled with all the colors of her crayon box. It also meant more playtime outside. As an adult, it meant more time to spend with Tanner after work and daycare—and more time to accomplish all her chores. At some level beyond her understanding, summer still infused her spirit with joy. And in spite of her misgivings concerning her family, that joy filled her now as she looked forward to when Noah would arrive at her apartment to take her and Tanner out to dinner.

CHAPTER TWO

As soon as Jo opened the door to their apartment after dinner, Tanner went straight to his toybox.

"Come play, Noah," he called over his shoulder.

Jo dropped into an armchair and motioned for Noah to join her son. She smiled at the two of them, so different but so perfect together. Tanner had red hair and green eyes along with a fair complexion sprinkled with freckles. Noah had dark brown hair and eyes and a dark tan. Both were healthy specimens. Tanner was an active little boy who had worked off his baby fat long ago. Noah worked out at least five times a week and sported a chiseled body.

As she watched them, her cell phone chirped. She frowned and stared at the number for a moment before she tapped to decline the call.

"Who was it?" asked Noah over his shoulder. When she didn't answer, he turned to face her.

The frown still in place, Jo hesitated before answering. "My...." She glanced at Tanner. "Beth. It was Beth."

"Your...." Noah glanced at Tanner as well. "Ah, right. Beth. But how? I didn't think she...they...knew your number or even where you live."

"They don't. Or rather they didn't. Paige is the only one who knows."

"Do you think she told Beth?"

"Surely not." Her phone chirped again. "Beth again."

"Maybe you should answer it. Something might be wrong. I'll get Tanner changed into his play clothes. Tanner? Want to help me pick out your play clothes?"

"Okay."

Tanner jumped up and Noah lifted him with an air toss, carried him into his bedroom, and closed the door behind them. Jo answered her phone.

* * *

"Beth? How did you get this number? And why are you calling me?" asked Jo.

"Well, hello to you too dear sister."

"Stop with the sarcasm and answer my questions."

"Testy, aren't you?"

"Beth…."

"All right, all right. I called because we need you. First off, Dad has had a stroke."

"Is he…?"

"He's not dead, and he only had to stay in the hospital a couple of days. None of the effects from the stroke are extreme. They could have been a lot worse, and we're thankful they aren't, but dealing with them is still bad enough for him and Mom and me. Best I can understand it, the stroke was in the right side of his cerebrum. He's not paralyzed, but his whole left side is weak, he's unsteady, and his vision is off. He keeps insisting he's fine and tries to do things he needs to have help with. He's also having trouble with his memory, and his temper flares more than usual. What's worse, he refused to go to a rehab facility and opted for home rehab. He's not being cooperative with that either."

"What about Mom?"

"That's the second part. You know she's never had the best of health or dealt well with stressful situations, especially health related. Even when we were sick as kids. Dad is making that worse. He's driving her crazy, and she can't do it all by herself. I've been helping, but I have a husband and a family. I can't do it all by myself either. Jo, we need you to help out."

"You don't think I have any responsibilities?"

"I guess you have a job, but you could take some sick leave, couldn't you?"

"I also have…."

"Have what?"

"Nothing. When did this happen?"

"Two weeks ago."

"And you're just now calling me?"

"At first, I thought we could manage on our own. As soon as I realized how difficult it would be, I would have called you if I had known your number. I didn't want to tell Paige why because I didn't want her to tell you until I could talk to you. I finally had to tell her why it was important for me to contact you now."

"And what made you think Paige would know?"

"Pshaw. Paige was…is still, I guess…your best friend. You told her everything. Why wouldn't you tell her? Her mom and our mom figured she knew where you lived and what your phone number was ever since you left, but she denied it for the longest."

"You could have found me before now if you had tried…if you had wanted to."

"We didn't think you wanted to be found."

"It's always on me, isn't it?"

"What's that supposed to mean?"

"Nothing. So you finally convinced Paige to give you my number."

"Yes, but I had to tell her about Dad to convince her we needed you. And that you needed to know about his situation. When can you be here?"

"I haven't said I would come. Just what is it you want me to do?"

"Somebody needs to stay with Mom and Dad all the time. We can't afford to hire someone for all the time, and I can't do it all by myself. I have little ones."

"I have…. If I decide to come, let me make a couple of things clear. I will not stay in that house twenty-four hours a day, and I will not stay there at night. If I come, I'll stay there during the daytime, and you can either stay at night, or you can pay a sitter to cover your time. If I decide not to come, I'll pay for someone to stay with them half the time. No discussion."

Beth didn't respond.

"Beth?"

"Fine. Where will you stay at night? At Paige's house?"

"Or at a hotel."

"That costs money."

"Yes, it does. How long I'll stay—if I come—will depend on what I find when I get there. And one other thing."

"What?"

"You had better make sure Mom and Dad know not to bring up my leaving or my reason for leaving. Understand?"

"I understand. I'll do my best. Jo, why are you so ill with me anyway?"

"Why? You think I didn't see you smirking while you inhaled your cereal that morning? While Dad same as disowned me? You were his pet, but I was your sister. I deserved better than that. I have things to do now. I'll let you know in the morning what I decide."

Jo disconnected and took several deep breaths as she tried to calm herself. She looked up to see Noah standing in the doorway holding Tanner.

"How long have you been standing there?"

"Just a second or two. What's the story?"

"The short story is that my…Art…had a stroke, and Beth and Gwen are not able to manage by themselves."

"They want you to come help."

"They do. Or at least Beth does."

"Are you going?"

"I don't know. I'll have to sleep on it."

"And Tanner?"

"If I go, he goes with me. I need to talk to Paige about that." Jo's phone chirped again. "Speaking of Paige." Jo accepted the call.

* * *

Jo spoke before Paige had a chance. "Why did you give Beth my number? A heads-up would have been good."

"What? You mean she's already called you? She promised she would wait until I could talk to you and explain."

"And you believed her?"

"I did. I'm sorry, Jo. How did the call go?"

"Not all that well. Did you know…Art…had a stroke?"

"Not until today."

"But Beth said it happened two weeks ago, and she'd been trying to get my number ever since then."

"Dear heart, she has been trying to get your number for years."

"That's what she said. You never told me."

"No point in upsetting you. At some point, Mama overheard me talking to you on the phone. She subsequently told Beth and Gwen. The rest is history. They didn't begin begging without ceasing until after Art's stroke. They didn't tell me why until today."

"Ironic that talking to me wasn't important enough for them to beg for my number until they needed my help. Doubly ironic that they need my help almost six years to the day after I needed them. How did they keep you from knowing he had a stroke?"

"It wasn't really their fault, although Beth or Mama could have called and told me. I've been locked in caregiver mode myself for the past two weeks. Roger brought a bacterial virus home from work, and we've all had it. I haven't been anywhere since he got sick until today. I was at Houston's Grocery when Beth saw me and pulled out all her tricks."

"Are you all over the virus? Or do you think it's still in the house?"

"Yes and no. We're all over it, and my cleaning lady and I together have disinfected every square inch of this house."

"Good."

"Why? You're coming, aren't you? And you want to stay here?"

"I'm not sure yet. If I do come, I don't want to put you out. I can stay at a hotel."

"Are you bringing Tanner?"

"Of course."

"Then you're not staying at a hotel. You wouldn't anyway for my part. But if you're bringing Tanner, you have to stay here. You'll need someone to look after him while you're at your parents' house. And Michael and Tabitha would love to have him as their guest. He's like an older brother to them. I would love to have you as my guest as well. Roger and Noah might even enjoy each other's company if he comes with you."

"I'm sure Noah would like that, but he has surgeries scheduled. It would just be Tanner and me."

"Plan on staying here then."

"Thanks, Paige. One other thing. About Tanner. I did tell Beth if I came, I'd stay in the daytime, and she could stay at night or pay someone to stay in her place. I do not want Tanner in that house."

"That's what I figured, too. One more child in this house will not be a problem. The three of them play well together and love each other."

"Michael and Tabitha are fortunate you could stay home with them."

"I know. I am, too. That was a big part of our parenting plan. Two children with a full-time mom until the second one entered first grade. So far, all has gone according to plan."

"Okay then, I'll call you in the morning to tell you my decision."

"Until then."

"Until then."

Jo disconnected the call and turned to Noah and Tanner who were now in the floor playing with Tanner's train set. Tanner jumped up, ran to her, and climbed into her lap.

"Mommy, are we going to Michael and Tabitha's house?"

"Maybe. Would you like that?"

"Yes! They've been to our house, but I've never been to their house. I can't wait!"

"Don't get too excited until Mommy decides. Okay?"

"Okay." Tanner scrunched up his face. "Mommy, will it be like a vacation?"

"Not exactly. If we do go, Mommy will be going to help an old friend during the daytime."

"Like going to work?"

"Exactly like that."

"Where will I stay?"

"You'll stay with Auntie Paige—and Michael and Tabitha."

"All day?"

"Yes, all day."

"Will you come home at night like from work?"

"You bet I will."

"Where will we sleep?"

"We'll both sleep at Auntie Paige's house."

"Yay!" Tanner slithered out of her arms and ran back to his train set.

"Tanner," said Noah, "I'm going to talk with your mom a minute, okay?"

"Okay."

* * *

Jo and Noah took a seat on either side of the island in the kitchen.

"If you're going to stay with Paige, should I know her last name—and her husband's name—in case I have trouble reaching you?" Jo smiled. "I don't need to know all your business, but you've never been away from home since we started seeing each other. I…I might worry."

"And I would appreciate it if you did. Her full name is Paige Winston Wallace. Her husband's name is Roger."

"Jo, on another nosey note, should you talk to your therapist before you make a final decision?"

"I know what Dr. Weber would say."

"Oh? She knows about…whatever the situation is?"

"Yes. She knows I miss them, and from time to time, she reminds me that at some point, I will probably need to face the past, face them."

"And?"

"And this is not how I imagined it."

"I could reschedule my surgeries and go with you."

"No. I don't want you to do that. Besides, as this would be my first time back in six years, there are bound to be fireworks. I'd rather you not be in the middle of that."

"I want to be there for you and with you, whenever, wherever, you need me."

"Noah—"

"I know. A conversation for another time. Be forewarned. I'm going to stick around until that time comes."

Noah reached out to take Jo's hand in his. She smiled at him, but she could not prevent the sadness she felt in her eyes.

"Noah, until I can face the past with them, I can't face it with you."

"Then I hope you decide to go."

This time her smile made it to her eyes.

"I'd better go now," said Noah. "I have a long day ahead of me, and it starts early. Let me know what you decide, and don't leave without stopping by the hospital."

"I will let you know, and I won't leave without seeing you."

At the door, Tanner jumped up into Noah's arms, and they hugged each other goodnight. "Noah," said Tanner, "when are you going to spend the night with me? My bed is big enough for both of us if we snuggle together."

"Maybe someday, Tanner, but not for a while. In the meantime, we can still have fun together when I am around."

"I know."

Noah hugged him tightly and kissed Jo on the cheek as he handed Tanner to her. He looked as if he wanted to hug her, too, but he held back.

After Noah left, Jo carried Tanner to the picture window to watch Noah leave. Tanner loved Noah. He also loved Noah's 2021 Matador Red Mica Lexus ES 250 F Sport All Wheel Drive and was fascinated by it—how it looked, how it ran, how it felt, how it smelled. He loved riding in it to the park and telling his friends its full name, which he practiced at home and every time he rode in it. Given a choice, Tanner would prefer to ride in the Lexus rather than in the Kia. As much as she loved her Kia, she didn't blame him. She loved riding in the Lexus, too.

* * *

After Noah left, Jo readied Tanner and herself for bed. When she leaned over to kiss him on the forehead, he patted her cheeks and said, "Mommy?"

"Yes, sweetheart?"

"I wish Noah could be my daddy."

"Sweet, sweet Tanner," she whispered as she brushed the hair out of his eyes. "Noah is a good man."

"He wishes he could be my daddy, too."

"Now what makes you say that?"

"He loves me. He smiles at me, and he rocks me to sleep sometimes. He takes me to the park, and he kisses my hurts when I fall down, just like you do. He loves you, too. His eyes get all sparkly when he looks at you. You know my friend Marty at daycare?"

"I do." She wrinkled her nose at what she thought was an abrupt change in subject.

"Marty has a daddy. His daddy is married to his mommy. If you married Noah, would he be my daddy?"

"Yes, if I married Noah, he would be your daddy."

"I hope you marry him soon. I want us to be together forever, and I don't want to get too old to have a daddy."

"You'll never get too old for that, Tanner. Now close your eyes and drift off to sleep."

Tears trickled down her cheeks as she watched Tanner's breathing slow into a sleep rhythm. When she was sure he was asleep, she kissed his cheek and whispered, "I wish I could marry him, Tanner, for both of us."

She eased out of Tanner's room into the living room and crossed over to the picture window to close the drapes. She stood for a moment looking out at the star-speckled night.

"Oh, Tanner, once upon a time, I thought I would marry the love of my life and live happily ever after. I looked forward to life and what it held. And then my world crashed and fell apart. Now just when I may be putting it back together and have let go enough to spend time with Noah, I may have to face it all over again. I'm not sure this is what Dr. Weber meant or how she envisioned it when she encouraged me to face my past. It certainly isn't how I envisioned it."

Jo glanced at the calendar hanging on the wall beside her. "Isn't that another bit of irony? I left home shortly before Father's Day six years ago. If I go back, I'll be returning shortly before Father's Day this year. Some fathers—birthfathers or not—deserve a day of celebration. Some do not."

CHAPTER THREE

Thursday, June 10, 2021

Jo awoke early the next morning, her decision made before she opened her eyes. After she called the head nurse to schedule her time off, she showered and dressed and packed for the trip before she roused Tanner.

As she went to close the last dresser drawer, she paused and laid her hand on her childhood diary, a birthday present when she turned thirteen. Her first entry was that night after her birthday party. Her last entry was the day after she arrived in Nashville after leaving her hometown near Knoxville. Beside her diary lay her more recent journal begun during an elective creative writing class at the end of her junior year at Vanderbilt University. She placed one hand on the two books. After the briefest of hesitations, she grabbed both and stuffed them into her largest suitcase under her clothes.

After dragging all of their luggage into the living room, she returned to awaken Tanner. Though sleepy-eyed, he jumped into her arms.

"Are we leaving now?"

"After breakfast and a bath. Tanner, while Mommy cooks breakfast, I want you to pack some of your toys for our trip. Your traveling toy bag is beside your toybox. You can take as many toys as will fit in the bag and three stuffed toys on top of the bag. Okay?"

"Okay, Mommy. Am I wearing jeans and a tee like yours? With my runners?"

Jo laughed. "You and Noah and your runners! Yes, I've already laid out your runners, your blue jeans, your navy T shirt, and your undies. Just like Mommy's."

Tanner made a face and shook his head. "No undies like Mommy's."

Jo picked him up and snuggled. "No, those are not like mine." They both giggled.

"Mommy, can we have pancakes for breakfast?"

"We can. They will be ready soon, so get to work." Jo set him on the floor, and they both got busy with their chores.

When they were ready, Jo left Tanner with the neighbor woman who had kept him since he was two months old while she worked and attended classes. Then she loaded everything into her silver Kia Rio. The Kia was five years old when she purchased it in 2018 at the end of her junior year, but she loved the one-owner five-door hatchback, and it had served her well.

Tanner had managed to fit enough toys in the canvas carryall that it was so heavy, she had to drag it down the stairs and out to the Kia. She filled the cargo area, the front passenger side, and the passenger side of the back seat area with their luggage, but she put only canvas clothing bags in the back seat and left ample space beside Tanner's car seat for his three stuffed toys.

When she returned for Tanner, he jumped up. "Can we go now?"

"We can after we both take a potty break."

Once they were both in the car and buckled in, she handed Tanner a sippy cup.

"Mommy, are we going to say goodbye to Noah?" he asked. "You said we would."

"Yes, we are. I've called him, and he's going to meet us in the parking lot. We won't get out, though. We'll just say goodbye."

"Okay."

* * *

Noah was waiting for them when they arrived at Vanderbilt University Medical Center. He kissed them both on the cheek. "Drive carefully. Call me when you get there. Call me if you need me. Call me…anytime."

Jo grinned at him. "I will. We'll miss you, too. And you can take care of yourself as well."

"Will do."

Noah walked back to the hospital and waved at them before entering the building. Jo started the Kia, but before she pulled out, she looked through the rearview mirror and asked, "Tanner, which playlist do you want to hear? Country, classical, spiritual, lullabies?"

He scrunched his face as he seriously considered his choice then smiled and said, "Country, please."

Her son never ceased to amaze her. He loved music as much as she did. All kinds of music. She shouldn't be surprised at his eclectic taste. After all, he was her son, and he had listened to all of her music choices for the nine months before he was born and for two years more before he started asking for certain music. She smiled at him, started the playlist, and pulled out of the parking lot. Then they were on their way. Tanner played quietly with his stuffed dinosaurs until he fell asleep.

I shouldn't go, thought Jo. *I'm finally reclaiming myself, and I'm afraid they will try to wear me down and destroy me again.*

* * *

As she drove I-40 and Tanner slept, Jo thought about how and why she had put this trip off and how it could have been too late. *Maybe it is too late. I don't want Dad to have another stroke. If I confront him and Mom, it could happen. What purpose would that serve? For that matter, what purpose would it serve if I confront Tanner's father?*

The overcast sky and the clouds threatened to dampen her spirits, but the rain held off, and she enjoyed the shades of green painting either side of the interstate like a protective barrier for her and Tanner.

As she drew closer to the small town in which she had grown up, her thoughts drifted back to her early years—and to Andrew Richards, the boy who lived next door. Andrew was born a month before Jo was. They had known each other before they had known anyone else except, of course, their parents and his older brothers, all of whom looked like their father, Frank. None of them had looked like their mother, Peggy, who Jo had always thought typified the term mousy.

Jo, Beth, and the Richards' boys had played together, gone to school together, attended the same small church, Agape Baptist Church, together all their lives. Both came from traditional southern Christian families—traditional if a little dysfunctional.

At the time, though, Jo never thought of her family as dysfunctional. They had done all the things families were supposed to do. Gone to church, on family picnics, on vacations. Had TV family nights and evening devotional times. Had neighborhood cookouts and dinner on the ground at church. Except dinner was no longer on the ground but on long tables in the church's fellowship hall.

In their neighborhood and at school, she and her sister Beth had both played softball. Their parents had attended all of the games, cheering them on as loudly as any other parents. And how many after-game hot dogs had the four of them consumed over the years? In church, she and Beth had been active in Mission Friends, Girls in Action, and Acteens.

Of course, they all had their own idiosyncrasies. She hadn't put words to it then, even recognized it, but Dad was demanding, controlling, and critical to the point of sometimes being demeaning. Mom was totally submissive. Whatever Dad said, she supported. Jo wondered now, though, if she had truly been submissive or just worn down. She and Beth had their own problems, sibling rivalry being just the tip of the proverbial iceberg.

Everything seemed to change—and not for the better— when Jo turned thirteen. That's the time she thought of after leaving Dr. Weber's office. She had become sullen, stubborn, headstrong, rebellious. Only at home though, never at school.

She knew it at the time, but she didn't understand it herself and seemed to have little if any control over it. Even then, though, she realized that the level of what her mom called teenage angst in her friends did not begin to compare to her own level of angst.

Nevertheless, they were happy, or so she had thought, at home and church, one an extension of the other. Andrew's family life was much the same as hers. She had taken for granted that all families were that way. Except Paige's family. Things were different at her house, calmer, more peaceful, even though Paige's mother worked outside the home.

Both Jo's and Andrew's mothers were stay-at-home moms, content to do so and happy they had that luxury. Both their fathers worked—Andrew's father in an office and her father in a factory—and were community leaders.

All four parents taught Sunday School at the only Baptist church in their small community. It, too, was traditional—or old-fashioned according to some. It even kept the old Sunday School divisions for children—Primary, Junior, Intermediate, and Senior. After nursery and pre-school, neither Andrew nor Jo knew any other Sunday School teachers except their parents. Andrew's mother taught the Primary class, Jo's mother the Junior class. Jo's father taught the Intermediate class, and Andrew's father the Senior class.

One of the recurring Sunday School lessons that all four parents had hammered home over the years was that they should forgive if they wanted to be forgiven.

If Jo had learned anything, however, during the last two months at home six years ago, it was that talking the talk and walking the walk were two entirely different things. Forgiving was the last thing on her mind when she left home.

Six years did not sound all that long ago, but to Jo it seemed a lifetime. A lifetime during which she wished she could tell them how sorry she was for any turmoil she had caused. A lifetime during which she had forgiven them for the turmoil they had caused.

All of them. Even though she doubted they felt any guilt whatsoever. But she hadn't forgiven them because she wanted to be forgiven or because they had said to do so. She had forgiven them because Jesus had said to do so. They were mere men. In the end, they could not shake her faith. She had also asked God to forgive them. If Jesus could ask God to forgive those who crucified Him, surely she could ask God to forgive those who had hurt her and broken her heart.

Jesus was the one stability in her life, though she was angry with Him at first until she realized it was displaced anger. She knew He had forgiven her for her own sins and failures, and she knew He wanted her to forgive those she had left behind. Not at first and not easily, but she finally did. She had to forgive for her own peace.

She did have peace, but the past still had a hold on her. On her life. Perhaps the reason she couldn't let go of the past and move forward was because they didn't know she had forgiven them or because they were unaware that they had done anything that needed forgiveness. They still might not accept her forgiveness or forgive her, but maybe going home, facing the past with each of them, would help her break that hold. Help her finally let go of her burden and truly place it in God's hands.

* * *

Though Jo's thoughts had been troubling, the transition from morning Nashville traffic to I-40 to the exit onto the country road that led to her small town had been pleasant enough with the mingled greens of summer, the colors of crops in the fields, and the comfortable temperature even with the threat of rain hanging in the overcast and cloudy skies.

As she drove through her hometown, she saw that nothing had changed in six years. She hoped that wasn't an omen. As she passed the theater, she exhaled a breath of relief. At least the movie on the theater marquee was a new one. Hopefully, that would nix the omen.

When she left the town proper and turned onto the street where Paige lived, the threatened raindrops spattered her windshield. *Oh well*, she thought, *at least we didn't have to drive in the rain.*

She turned into Paige's drive, came to a stop behind the 2019 Abyss Blue Pearl Subaru Ascent SUV, and smiled. She teased Paige often enough about her family car, but she actually liked the SUV. Someday, when she could afford it, she would like to get an SUV, too, but not one as new as Paige's.

By the time Jo lifted Tanner from his car seat, Paige was beside her. Paige had been her best female friend since kindergarten. Dressed in her signature jean shorts, red T shirt, and sandals, she had changed little over the years except, of course, for filling out and getting taller, although she was still only an inch taller than Jo. Her straight black hair and light olive skin tone came from her mother's side of the family. Her smattering of freckles came from her father's side.

After a brief hug, Jo handed Tanner off to Paige and began unloading her Kia. As she grabbed her last load and locked the doors, thunder and lightning split the sky—and darkened Jo's mood. She looked up and said to the storm and the heavens, "I hope this isn't another omen." As she sprinted for the house, she thought of Noah and added an afterthought. "His extra set of hands would have been nice. Maybe someday."

Inside, she carried her last load to the room where she and Tanner would sleep and dried off her luggage and herself with the large fluffy towel Paige had left on the bed.

When she returned to the living room where all three kids watched TV, she found Tanner burrowing into one corner of the sofa. As soon as he saw her, he jumped off the sofa and ran into her arms.

"Mommy, I'm scared."

She had no doubt he was. A different town. A different house. And a storm. Jo was a little scared, too. She hugged him close and said, "We're okay, Tanner. We're inside Auntie Paige's house. We're dry. And I seem to remember that Auntie Paige said she would have chocolate cupcakes waiting for us."

Tanner lifted his head from her shoulder. His eyes opened wide. "With icing on them?"

They both looked at Paige. Her eyes lit up.

"Of course, with icing on them! Come on kiddos. Let's have a welcome-to-our-house snack with cupcakes and milk."

Soon the storm outside was all but forgotten. The one in Jo's head and heart had not let up, though. She dreaded the day ahead.

* * *

That night, after turning out all but the bedside lights, she tucked Tanner into bed and sat beside him until he fell asleep. Then she went to her suitcase and pulled out a gown and robe. Her fingers touched the diary and the journal lying underneath them. After a moment's hesitation, she pulled them out along with her night clothes.

After finishing her night-time routine, she picked up the diary and the journal and crawled into bed. She leaned back against the wall and closed her eyes. So much had happened during the years between her last diary entry and her last journal entry—including her visits with Dr. Weber.

She hadn't started seeing Catherine Weber until the end of her junior year. Until Tanner was a little over two years old. She was too focused on caring for her baby, studying for her classes, and working to think about anything or anyone else. Not to mention being too scared. She didn't go out or socialize. She did attend church services but not Sunday School classes. She avoided making friends. Some of the young men at church and at school would ask her out, but she had no desire to date. She would shudder at the thought. She would draw up inside and get sick to her stomach whenever they approached her.

Then one of the women in her creative writing class read her poem aloud in class—a poem about her own experiences—that both upset and inspired Jo. The poem and her journaling led her to compare her life to that of the woman who wrote the poem and to realize that she needed help to come to terms with all that had—or had not—happened.

She had chosen Dr. Weber for that help because, though she was a psychotherapist, she was also a psychiatrist and had been through both medical school and psychiatric residency.

Even then she didn't see her because she was ready to have a relationship or even date casually. She saw her because she didn't want to be controlled by her emotions, her anxiety, her experiences. She made progress and in time was able to socialize more comfortably, although she still had her issues, and she still had no desire to date. She figured that was just as well. She didn't have the time to spare.

Then she met Noah—actually met him. She had first seen him in the hospital at the beginning of her first year of her MSN program, but she had never spoken to him. She thought he was handsome and knew he was adored by all of the female nursing staff and his patients. She soon learned that he was a surgeon, which of course, meant he was older than she was but not that much older.

Apparently, he had noticed her, too, because by the time he had asked her out, he had done his homework and had discovered that she had a son, she never dated, and she was hesitant at best around men. He had also discovered quite by accident that she was one of Dr. Weber's patients. He was walking down the hallway discussing a mutual patient with another physician when Jo arrived for an appointment with Dr. Weber. They spoke to each other, but neither had ever mentioned that day.

She suspected that it was because of what he had learned that he had made her acquaintance and spoken to her often before asking her to meet him for coffee in the hospital cafeteria. They then met for coffee several times before he asked her on a date. He had been taking down the brick wall she had built around herself and Tanner one brick at a time.

They had finally gone on their first date a little over a year ago, right after she had finished the first year of her MSN program. He had met Tanner soon after. They had begun attending church together, sometimes at her church, sometimes at his. She wondered if any of that would have happened if it had not been for the creative writing class.

* * *

Jo opened her eyes and opened the journal to the page she had marked three years ago. She silently reread the poem that she had recorded because she didn't want to forget.

Whittlings

I recoiled from the brown, weathered hands
and peered sideways at the wrinkled face.
I pretended I didn't hear him
and felt guilty without knowing why.
I didn't cry until long after.
Only a touch and a few words. But

each time they whittled away a part
of what was me—much as he whittled
on his walking sticks. No one knew but
the two of us. As I got older,
I was able to avoid the touch

but never the words. His words were there—
on his lips—in his eyes—forever
asking me—making me promise not
to tell. He said no one would ever

understand. They would put him away.
When I broke my promise, I found out
he was right. No one understood. But

he wasn't put away. He was old
and it was long ago. And no one
said any words to me or touched me.

And I felt a little more of what
once was me being whittled away.

Jo traced the words on the page and blinked back tears. She closed the journal and opened her diary to the last entry, the one she had written the day after she left home six years ago.

It happened two months ago. I prayed I wouldn't get pregnant. I was terrified. For the baby. For myself. For the reactions of those I loved. I couldn't be sure because of my irregular cycles. But after two months and not a hint of a period, I had to face the possibility. Day before yesterday, Saturday, I bought a pregnancy test. I resisted taking the test until Sunday night. When I finally took it, I realized my worst fears.

I cried myself to sleep and woke up yesterday morning with swollen, red eyes and a throbbing headache. When I went down to breakfast, Mom and Dad already knew. Mom had found the pregnancy test in my wastebasket. They were waiting for me. I tried to talk to them. They wouldn't listen. I left and went to Paige's house. I called Andrew to meet me there, but when he came, he wouldn't listen either.

I can't write the words to describe all that was said or all that happened with Mom and Dad or with Andrew, but I will never forget.

Afterwards, Paige took me to the bank, and I withdrew all of my savings, money intended to help with college for expenses my scholarships might not cover. I took part of it and bought a bus ticket to Nashville. I stayed at the Y last night.

Today, I found a two-bedroom apartment close to Vanderbilt University. It's small but nice and in a good neighborhood. And it has appliances, so I'll only have to buy a few pieces of furniture. I bought a sleeping bag for tonight. I'm exhausted. I'll look for cheap furniture tomorrow. And I'll find a part-time job somewhere. I will not let what has happened prevent me from going to school. Somehow and some way, I will survive this.

Jo closed her diary and her eyes. She had survived, but the events of those two days still haunted her and poisoned the memory of what had once been her home, her safe place, her happy place. Certainly, there was turmoil and dysfunction, but it had been home. She lost herself as her mind drifted back six years to the morning she had walked out of that home, out of that life, back to the words and actions she couldn't bring herself to write in her diary.

CHAPTER FOUR

J o had hoped against hope that she wouldn't get pregnant, but she had feared it for two months. She hadn't purchased the pregnancy test until the previous Saturday. She couldn't make herself take the test until Sunday night. And then she knew. She didn't know what or how she would tell her parents and Andrew. She had worried and cried throughout the night. She finally fell asleep sometime after two in the next morning and then overslept.

When Jo finally awoke, she knew she could never tell her parents or Andrew the truth. She could not destroy hers and Andrew's families whether they believed her or not. And she could not marry Andrew and keep such a secret from him.

She still didn't know what she would tell them, but she couldn't tell them the truth. Maybe she wouldn't tell them anything. She would soon be leaving for Nashville and Vanderbilt University. She could have the baby and give it up for adoption, and no one would ever know. Before she left, she could break hers and Andrew's engagement. She could tell him she wanted to finish her education and see the world. She would tell him she cared for him but not enough to give up the future she wanted.

Jo had cried so long and so hard the night before, she had awoken with swollen, red eyes and a headache. She covered the red under her eyes with concealer thinking she would get out of the house before her parents noticed. Then she would talk to Paige and figure out what to do before she told anyone else anything—or simply left.

As she staggered in and out of her bathroom, she didn't notice that her wastebasket had been emptied. She knew her mother often entered her room while she slept to collect her trash, but she didn't remember that it was trash collection day. Not until she walked into their bright, cheerful little kitchen.

Beth sat at the breakfast table with a smirk on her face. Jo's trash bag sat on the floor beside their mother. The pregnancy test lay on top of it.

Then Jo remembered collection day, and she knew that part of her decision had already been made for her. Even so, she could not have imagined or prepared herself for what happened next.

Her mother spoke first, her eyes filled with tears and disappointment. "When were you going to tell us?" she asked.

Before Jo could answer, her mother threw another question at her. "How could you do this to us, to Andrew's parents? What were you thinking?"

Jo stood there, tongue-tied. Her mother was usually the calm, dispassionate one. She looked at her father, hoping for support but not expecting it. The look in his eyes was beyond disappointment. His eyes were filled with fury. His face was redder than she had ever seen it. He gritted his teeth as he spit his first question at her.

"Why couldn't you wait until after you married? Does Andrew know yet? If not, you can rest assured, I will tell him…that and a lot more! You've always been stubborn," he growled. "Headstrong, pushing the envelope. But this…when…when did you become a tramp?"

"Mom. Dad. That's not what happened."

"Oh? You'd have us believe it was an immaculate conception?"

"No, Dad. That's not what I meant. Please. Let me explain." Whatever made her think he would give her a chance to explain? He never had before. He didn't then.

"We know how girls get pregnant."

"Dad—"

"Stop. No more. I don't want to hear it. You can forget about me paying for a college education. If you're old enough to get pregnant, you're old enough to get a job. If Andrew is any man at all, he'll marry you, and you can both get jobs to support this child."

"Dad, it wasn't Andrew!" she blurted out before she could stop herself.

"What? It wasn't even the man you planned to marry? You committed adultery before you even married him? How could you do that to him? To your mother? To me?"

He drew back and struck her so hard across her face that she fell to the floor. He had spanked her before, even slapped her, but never that hard.

She stared up at him as he glared down at her.

"You little Jezebel, hussy, trollop. "You…harlot!" When he spoke again, his growl turned menacing. "If you're going to demean yourself, you're not going to do it again while living in my house. You have one week to find a job and a place to live."

Finally, Jo pushed herself up off the floor and stood trembling, her mouth open, not believing what was happening. And then, something snapped inside her.

She whispered, "I won't need a week."

She turned and bolted up the stairs and into her room, slammed her door, and locked it behind her. She pulled out her luggage and stared at the bags. She couldn't walk to Paige's carrying them. Through blinding tears, she managed to call a taxi and then leave a message for Andrew to meet her at Paige's house. Finally, she threw what belongings she could, what few books she could, along with her diary and her engagement ring, into a single large suitcase and a single overnight bag. She jerked her door open and flew down the stairs, dragging her bags behind her. Her father blocked her way.

"If you leave like this, you don't ever come back."

She took a deep breath and whispered, "Get out of my way." Without another word to him or her mother, she raced out of the house just as the taxi pulled up.

Once inside the taxi, all Jo could do was shake her head in disbelief at what she had done. Not about the scene with her parents but about calling Andrew. Why had she bothered? What purpose would it serve? Whatever would she say to him?

She should have just left and sent him a Dear John letter. It would have been easier for both of them.

But she had called him, and he was standing in front of the porch steps waiting for her. Paige leaned against a porch pillar, her arms wrapped around her body, a frown on her face.

"Jo," said Andrew as he stepped toward her, "what's wrong? Why were you crying? And why do you have your luggage?"

He tried to put his arms around her. Jo pulled away.

"Jo?"

All reason about what she should say left her. Her body jerked as she sobbed. "Andrew, I'm sorry. I'm pregnant. And my dad threw me out of the house."

"That's not possible." He glanced at Paige but continued. "We were together only once, and I used protection. If you're pregnant, it can't be mine." He stared at her. "Whose is it, Jo? Who else have you been with?"

Jo's sobs diminished into hiccups as she absorbed the meaning of his words. "You're accusing me of being unfaithful, too? Andrew, I thought we knew each other better than that. You're right. It's not yours. And I'm leaving town. I shouldn't have called you. I'm here to ask Paige to take me to the bus station. And…and…we're not getting married!"

"No. Wait. You don't know what you're saying. I don't know what I'm saying. We need to talk about it. Please, Jo."

He reached out for her. She again pulled away as she wiped the tears from her eyes.

"Leave me alone, Andrew. Leave. Now. I…I…don't want to see you anymore."

His words had broken her heart. The hurt on his face broke it even more. She wanted to rush into his arms. She couldn't. She refused to watch as he got into his car and drove away.

After Jo had told Paige everything and had cried out what tears she had left, Paige took her to the bank and to the bus station. Jo left and never looked back. She knew she could never go home again.

CHAPTER FIVE

Thursday, June 10, 2021

Jo wiped the flood of tears from her eyes. That day, the day she had left home forever, was six years ago almost to the day. Tanner was now five. She was twenty-four.

She had accomplished a lot in those six years. Everything she had set out to do in fact. Four years after leaving, she had earned her BA in Biological Sciences with a pre-nursing program of study from Vanderbilt University College of Arts and Sciences.

At the beginning of her second year in Vanderbilt University's Master of Science in Nursing degree program, she had passed the NCLEX-RN and applied for and received her RN license. This past May, scarcely a month ago, she had graduated with her MSN degree and then passed the exam and received her AANP FNP certification. She had been working full time at Vanderbilt University Medical Center ever since graduation.

She had no illusions about how fortunate she had been. She had come to Nashville with scholarships in hand, with savings she had accumulated over the years from her babysitting jobs to her part-time jobs after school and on weekends. She had managed to work part time during her entire six years at Vanderbilt University except for the two months after Tanner was born. And she had taken advantage of every opportunity available, including WIC for Tanner. It had not been easy, and it had been necessary—as her grandmother used to say—"to pinch every penny until it hollered."

The one thing she hadn't done was exorcise her demons. She had made progress, though. She and Tanner had survived the old life and had a new life before them. She loved Tanner unconditionally. She loved Noah secretly. Tanner loved Noah, and Noah loved him as much as he loved her.

And now this. How could her family expect her to come home? Why would they even want her to? Of course, they had no idea how fortunate she was that the head nurse valued her enough to grant her a leave of absence to help take care of her father.

Jo turned out the bedside light. She slept fitfully, replaying her memory from that day six years ago over and over and dreading a repeat when she saw her parents for the first time since that morning.

* * *

Friday, June 11, 2021

At seven o'clock the next morning, Jo hugged Tanner long enough that he began to squirm.

"I need to go play, Mommy. Michael and Tabitha are waiting for me."

"All right already." Jo grinned and kissed his forehead. "Go play." She set him down and watched him run into the living room to plop down on the floor with his playmates. "I'll see you this evening, Tanner," she called to him.

"See you, Mommy."

In spite of her own misgivings at leaving him, she was thankful that he was secure enough to know she would return at the appointed time.

She hugged Paige and left for her parents' house. How would she react? How would they react? Did they even know she was coming? She knew she had changed. She wondered if they had changed, too.

When she turned onto the street where her parents lived, she was overcome by her sense of déjà vu. She may have changed, but her childhood neighborhood, set within the town proper, had not changed. Most of the homes were older two-story structures with attached garages and just enough space between them for double hedgerows to separate the individual lots. Some homes were larger than others. Some lots were larger than others. But all were quaint and spoke of a simpler time.

As soon as she turned into her parents' driveway, she saw that her dad's old beat-up black pickup truck still sat in the garage while the family station wagon sat behind it in the driveway. She smiled. Some things hadn't changed for her parents, either. Dad was practical if anything, and Mom said a car was a car. Any vehicle was fine with her as long as it got her where she wanted to go and back home again.

Beth had parked on the side of the street, leaving Jo just enough room to pull her Kia in behind the station wagon. She wondered if it had been intentional.

"I doubt it. I can't imagine her making things easier for me."

Jo stepped out of her Kia and gripped the door, frozen in place, staring at what had once been her safe place, her home.

* * *

At the front door, Jo raised her hand to knock. Beth opened the door before she could, and Jo took another step into the past. Still maybe half an inch shorter than Jo, Beth had the same golden-brown hair as Jo except she had always worn it short because it was curly like their mother's. She also had the same dark amber eyes as Jo, again like their mother's. Jo's hair was straight like her father's, although both his hair and eyes were dark brown.

After a brief moment of staring at each other, Beth spoke first. "I was beginning to wonder if you were going to make it—or back out."

"Good morning to you, too," said Jo. "It's nice to see you after six years. How are you doing?"

"Don't be sarcastic. What would you expect after six years?"

"You're right. How silly of me. Did you tell Mom and Dad I was coming?"

"I did."

"Are they as thrilled as you are?' Jo knew she needed to drop the sarcasm, but she was having trouble doing so.

"They are apprehensive, as you might expect, but they do understand what a strain this has put on me. They are glad you agreed to help. Come on in then. Let's get this over with. I need to go home."

Jo followed her sister into the living room. Her mother, as slender and feminine as ever, stood wringing her hands as she waited for them. She leaned as if she were about to take a step toward Jo but stopped short of doing so. Her greeting was robotic at best.

"Jo. It was good of you to come. Art and I are glad to see you. Did you have a pleasant trip?"

"Thank you, Mom. It's nice to see you and Dad, too. I did have a pleasant trip."

"Then you arrived before the thunderstorm hit?"

"I pulled into Paige's driveway just as it started."

"I'm glad you didn't have to drive in it."

"Me, too."

Jo flinched when she looked beyond her mom to where her dad sat in a wheelchair, his back stiff and his hands clenched. He had always been such a robust and healthy man. He had lost weight and looked almost frail. He had not turned his attention from the morning news. She stepped into the living room between him and the TV.

"Dad, how are you feeling today?"

He frowned at her. "I'm feeling as well as I was yesterday, better than I was two weeks ago. As if you cared."

"Dad, I didn't know about your stroke until this past Wednesday. I'm here now. I can help."

"You wouldn't know what to do. Gwen and Beth know what to do. The home health nurse knows what to do. The therapist knows what to do."

"Dad, I know what to do, also. I'm a registered nurse now. And I'm here to help."

Art blinked and pulled back. "Humph. Maybe you can be of some help then." He twisted the edges of the blue and red knitted afghan draped over his lap. "I hope you don't expect us to forgive you for what you did."

"Dad, we've all done things to be sorry for."

"We've not done anything to be sorry for."

"Right. Just know, when you realize that it works both ways, that you've already been forgiven. I forgave you long ago for what you did. And if you ever find it in your heart to forgive me, know that I am sorry for whatever I did to upset you and Mom or make your lives miserable that day or any of the days before it."

"But you moved forward without a thought for us. If you were sorry for anything, why did it take you this long to return home?"

"Dad, I have moved forward, beyond the past. But I never stopped thinking about you and Mom. Still, even though I'd moved forward, I could not truly face the past or those from it who still haunted me. You, on the other hand, apparently have remained in the past. You have never forgiven me for what I did—or for what you imagined I did. Hopefully, someday you will and will also understand it all."

"Whatever. Don't think you're going to tell me what to do while you're here."

"Dad, I could have been coming home for your funeral. I'm thankful that was not the case. The next time, it could be just that. Is that what you want? To die before our family has a chance to heal? If not, you have to listen to Mom and to the doctor and to the nurses. I don't care if you listen to me, but you have to listen to them. For your sake and for Mom and Beth's sakes."

Art shrugged and looked away. "We have a routine."

"Fine. Mom and I will discuss all that the doctor has said, and we'll do what we need to do. We'll follow your routine."

"Then may I finish watching the news now?"

"Yes, Dad." Jo heaved her shoulders in a sigh and turned to Gwen. "Mom, how about you and I have a cup of coffee?"

"Yes, that would be good. And we can go over the doctor's orders. Art, you call me—us—if you need anything." He shrugged again but didn't otherwise acknowledge even his wife. Gwen turned back to her daughters. "Beth, would you like to join us?"

"No, Mom, not this time. You and Jo need some time together, and I need to get home." She gave both of her parents a peck on the cheek and nodded at Jo before she left.

Jo bit her lip to keep from speaking but did nod in return before following her mom to the kitchen. She hoped their time together was better than the moments between her and her dad.

* * *

That evening, Jo glanced at the wall clock in the hallway. It was seven o'clock. She sighed with relief. Beth would arrive in about half an hour. It had been a long day and a productive one but not an overly difficult one.

The day had included visits from both her dad's home health nurse and his physical therapist. Jo had spent the day making herself acquainted with the two workers, observing and helping them, and filling in the missing pieces of what she had learned from her mom that morning.

She and her parents had avoided personal conversations, partly by being busy, partly by watching the TV at mealtimes. She did feel discouraged that she had felt more like a nurse than a daughter, more like she was visiting a patient than her parents. But she would give it time.

She heard a car door slam and looked out the peephole of the front door.

Beth is a little early, she thought. *That surprises me.* She opened the door.

"I know I'm a little early, but I wanted a few minutes alone with you before you left. How did it go today?"

Jo gave her a rundown of the day's events.

"Good that you had the distractions today. Let me say hello to the folks, and I'll walk out with you."

After Beth's hellos and Jo's goodbyes—which met with rebuff from her father but some good will from her mother— Beth followed Jo to the Kia.

"Okay, Beth. What's up?"

"I wanted to mention this, even though I was a little reluctant. But my husband—Alex Dalton—you remember him, don't you?"

"I do."

"He said I should go ahead and mention it while I had the chance." Beth frowned. "Jo, you have no idea what it's been like. One of the biggest things is the holidays. Mom no longer takes her turn having the aunts and uncles and their families at her house for any of the holidays. Her turn has fallen to me. Do you have any idea what a responsibility that is? If you had been here, we could have done it together, and it would have been easier. I'm beginning to dread the holidays."

Jo laughed.

"What's funny about that?" Beth planted her hands on her hips. "I'm serious."

"I'm sure you are. You have no idea yourself, do you?"

"What are you talking about?"

"When I was fifteen, a week before Thanksgiving, Mom told me she couldn't do the holidays anymore, and I would have to do them when it came her turn. I knew that whoever hosted did all the cooking and everything. I had no idea why. Mom said everyone pretended it was because each of them wanted everything done their own way, but she thought it was more because if all the women came to the kitchen, all the men followed them, and there was no room to do anything. Whatever the reason, I tried to do and oversee everything and everyone like Mom would have done it. It was still her house, and I wanted to do that for her—her way. But I was fifteen! I was overwhelmed, and no one ever offered to help even though I was as young as I was. I figured either they thought I had the same reason they did, or they thought I was just helping Mom. On top of that, every holiday that it fell to us, I did something that upset someone. Every. Single. Time. I came to hate the holidays. So, yes, I do have an idea of the responsibility and the stress and the aftermath."

"I never knew."

"How could you? You were thirteen and outside playing with the cousins, where I should have been. I am sorry all of that has fallen to you. As it is unlikely that I will ever be here for the holidays, let me make a couple of suggestions."

"By all means. Please do."

"Make your own holiday traditions. Suggest to the family that instead of one person or family doing all the work each time, you should have a potluck each holiday. Or as a last resort, when it's your turn, have the meals—something special—catered or take everyone out to a restaurant. I'll wager some of the family will look forward to your time as host. Worst case scenario, stop going and enjoy the day with your immediate family."

"That last one won't work. I do like your other ideas, though. All of them. I'll think on it. I'm glad I brought it up. I'm glad to know it didn't happen to just me. I'm sorry it happened to you, too, especially when you were that young."

"I'm glad you brought it up, too."

"Why didn't you ever say anything?"

"I don't know. I guess partly because I was doing it for Mom but partly because I couldn't believe everyone dumped all of the work on one person every holiday and blamed it on the women wanting to do everything their own way."

For the first time in so long, Jo and Beth hugged each other, and Jo left with a small but welcome lift to her spirits.

CHAPTER SIX

Saturday, June 12, 2021

As she left Paige's the next morning, Jo thought about the topics she and her parents had managed to avoid the day before. *I wonder which if any will come up today*, she thought. She didn't have to wait long to find out.

As soon as Beth left, Jo locked the door and crossed the hallway to the living room where her mom and dad watched the morning news together.

"Good morning, Mom. Good morning, Dad."

As soon as she spoke, her dad pointed the remote at the TV and clicked it off. He turned his head toward her and scowled. "What did you do with the baby?" he asked.

Jo threw her shoulders back and blinked her eyes at him. "What did I do with the baby? Is that all you can think to ask?"

"We always assumed you would have an abortion, even though you weren't raised that way."

"Or would give it up for adoption," added her mom. "You didn't mention it yesterday."

Jo walked into the living room and sat in the armchair closest to the doorway.

"We were busy yesterday. But you didn't ask yesterday. And *it* was a boy. I didn't abort him, although I did almost lose him, and I didn't give him away."

"What are you saying?" Her dad had lowered his voice, but he still glowered at her.

"I kept him. His name is Tanner."

"Oh, Jo," said Gwen, "where is he? Did you leave him with someone in Nashville?"

"No, I didn't leave him."

"Then where is he?" asked Art. "Not that we want to see him, of course."

"Of course not. That's why he's not here. He's at Paige's. He's playing with her children."

"Paige. Has she known all along?"

"As if it matters, yes, she has. I asked her not to tell you."

"That was thoughtless of you," said her dad, "but nothing more than we would have expected."

"That was thoughtless? Of me? Dad, you knocked me down and kicked me out of the house."

Art glared at her but did not respond.

Gwen cleared her throat and slipped closer to the edge of the sofa before speaking. "Art, Jo, that's all in the past now. The child is a part of Jo. He's a part of us. I would like to meet our first grandchild, our first grandson."

"Mom, his birth is in the past, but a lot of that past remains to haunt the present. We need to address it, but it's too soon. When we can address it—civilly—I'll decide whether or not I want you to meet Tanner."

"But he is our grandson."

"And he is my son. Now, we have a full day ahead of us. After I help you with your housework, Dad and I will do physical therapy—according to his therapist's instructions."

Art snorted.

"Art, you promised," said her mom.

"I'll do what the therapist said and no more."

"You do want to get out of that wheelchair, don't you?"

"Yes."

"Then do what Jo tells you to do."

Jo nodded at her mom in appreciation and then said, "Speaking of that wheelchair, why didn't you get a motorized wheelchair? It would have been easier on both of you."

"My doctor said he couldn't approve it because I wasn't able to safely get in and out of it without help. And as it costs more, my portion would be more," grumbled her father.

"That makes sense, but from what I've seen, you've made enough progress for him to reconsider it. When he does, I'll help cover your portion of the cost."

Art raised one eyebrow. "You make a lot of money, do you?"

Jo smiled. Her dad had always preached at her and Beth to find a job that paid well. "Not a lot of money, but I do okay, and I still have a little in savings."

Gwen shook her head. "I don't know how you managed."

"It wasn't easy, Mom, but I did. Now, let's get to work."

When they were far enough away from the living room that Art couldn't hear them, Jo took her mother's hand in hers and said, "Mom, I've arranged for the sitter you use when Beth has to be away to stay with Dad tomorrow so I can go to church with Paige. Beth said he was a good sitter and Dad likes him."

"He is, and Dad does, but it's too expensive. We can't afford it."

"I'm paying for it. You could go to church, too, if you want to."

"I would like to. Thank you. I'll decide in the morning."

* * *

That evening when Jo came back downstairs after putting up the last load of laundry, she heard Peggy talking in the living room. She caught her breath in a panic and considered leaving without saying goodbye. But she couldn't. Beth was standing in the hallway waiting for her and furiously tapping her foot.

"Beth? What's wrong?"

"Mom called me while you were doing therapy with Dad," said Beth. "You had a son, and you kept him. You could have told me."

Before Jo could respond, Peggy flew off the sofa into the hallway.

"You have a son? The one you were pregnant with when you left home? Is he Andrew's? If he is, Frank and I have a right to see him. Andrew has a right to see him."

After taking several deep breaths, Jo managed to say, "I never said he was Andrew's. And no, you do not have a right to see him. Beth, I will talk to you later." Jo grabbed her bags, which she had left beside the front door, and called out to her parents, "Mom, Dad, I'm leaving now." She hurried out of the house, jumped into her Kia, and drove away as fast as she could.

* * *

After she and Paige cleaned up the kitchen that night, Jo said, "Paige, I need to pick up a couple of things at our local box store."

Tanner, who had returned to ask for a sippy cup, jumped up and down. "Mommy, I want to go, too. I need a truck."

Jo smiled. "I'm sure you do. There aren't enough toys scattered all over Auntie Paige's house."

"Jo," said Paige, "I need to pick up a few things, too. Or do you need some alone time?"

"A few minutes would be fine. We could go together. You and yours could shop together. Tanner and I could shop together."

"You think that will be enough alone time?"

"If not, Tanner and I can go for a short drive later."

"It's Saturday night. We shouldn't run into anyone you know. If we do, you may have to make it a long drive."

"Let's hope not!"

* * *

Jo had picked up her necessary items, including the toy truck, and she and Tanner were headed to the checkout when she heard a familiar voice calling her name. She pressed her lips together, closed her eyes, and whispered, *Please, Lord, help me hold my tongue.* She turned around to face the voice, trying to block Tanner from the woman's view.

"Jo, I thought that was you. I heard you were in town. You remember me, don't you? I was Tracey Morgan. I don't know whether or not you know it, but if you and Paige have kept up with each other like Peggy thinks you have, I guess you do know. Andrew and I married a couple of years after you left."

"Yes, I remember you." Tracey had been a thin, prissy little girl with a child's voice, blue eyes, and bouncy blond Shirley Temple curls. She hadn't changed much at all except for her more matronly figure. "And I knew you and Andrew had married." Jo's attention was drawn to the boy sitting in Tracey's cart. Her jaw dropped. At that same instant, she felt Tanner grab her arm and peek around her.

Tracey's jaw dropped, too, as she stared at Tanner before glaring at Jo. "You lied. You both lied. You told your parents it wasn't Andrew's. Andrew said it wasn't his."

"Andrew wasn't lying," said Jo.

"You're lying now. Look at him." She pointed at Tanner. "Look at them." She pointed to her own son. "He looks…just like…Adam. He looks just like Andrew's pictures when he was that age. How could you?"

"I didn't."

"The proof is sitting right there in front of both of us. One thing's for sure. That also proves you came home for the very reason I suspected. You came here hoping to break up mine and Andrew's marriage. On top of that, you not only left Andrew without a word, but you took the engagement ring he had given you. Do you know how much that ring cost? How long it took him to save enough to buy me a ring?"

Jo wasn't sure how her supposed plan to break up their marriage led to the missing engagement ring, but she addressed both if briefly. "I know how much the ring was worth." She had wanted to keep her engagement ring to remind her she had once loved and been loved. But when she had to have a C-section because of complications and couldn't work for two months, she had to sell it to feed herself and Tanner. However, that was none of Tracey's business. "As for my coming back home, that had nothing to do with you or Andrew. I came back because my father had a stroke, and my mother isn't well or strong, and my sister couldn't manage it all by herself. She has a family to care for." She couldn't keep the sarcasm out of her voice on the last comment. "Regardless of all that, I do not want to have any part of this conversation here or now." She tipped her head toward Tanner expecting the woman to understand and be considerate. Her expectations were wrong again.

"Don't try to put me off. If Andrew and I weather through this, I have no doubt he will fight you for joint—"

"Tracey!" Paige pushed her way between the two buggies with her own. "How nice to see you. Jo, my kids are getting cranky. Here are my keys. How about you take the kids to the SUV, and I'll pay for all of our purchases. We can settle up later." She grabbed her few items and threw them into Paige's buggy.

Jo didn't take the time to respond. She took Paige's keys, grabbed Tanner, put him in the buggy with Michael and Tabitha, and flew out of the store.

None of the children said a word until she had them all fastened in their booster seats. As she slid into the passenger side seat, Tanner spoke up quietly.

"Mommy, why did that lady get mad at me?"

Jo turned around to face the children. "Oh, Tanner, she wasn't mad at you. She just happened to look your way when she got mad at Mommy."

"Why was she mad at you? And who is Andrew?"

"It was about something that happened years ago before you were born. And Andrew…Andrew is her husband. He has nothing to do with us. Hey, guys, I see Paige has a box of animal crackers up here. Anybody want one?"

A unified "Yes!" greeted her.

"Coming right up."

Jo hoped the crackers would hold them until they got home and help them forget the encounter with Tracey. She also hoped Andrew would not approach her with Tracey's accusations.

CHAPTER SEVEN

Sunday, June 13, 2021

The next morning as Jo and Tanner walked down the stairs ready for church, they heard a knock at the front door. Jo looked at Paige who was standing in the hallway with her kids waiting for her husband.

"Who?"

"I have no idea," said Paige. "We're not expecting anyone. Kids, all three of you, into the living room to play, but do not get dirty or wrinkled."

Tanner jumped off the last step and followed the other two into the living room.

Paige went to the door and opened it. Andrew stood there with a frown on his face. His gaze went directly from Paige to Jo standing behind her at the bottom of the stairs. He pushed his way past Paige and yelled at Jo.

"Where is he? You said he wasn't mine. I didn't think he could be mine. It was one time, and I used protection. I want to see him."

Tanner darted into the hallway and grabbed Jo around her legs. "Mommy, why is that man yelling at you?"

"He's upset, Tanner, but everything will be all right. Go play with your friends. Paige will stay with you. I need to speak to this man before we leave." Tanner hesitated. "It's okay, baby. Go on now." She lifted his hands and placed one of them in Paige's hand. Andrew moved to follow them, but Jo grabbed his arm and said, "No."

Paige took Tanner back to the living room where all three children watched as Jo led the angry man to the front porch.

"Jo, he looks just like my son Adam and even favors my daughter Ellen. He has to be mine. Now Tracey is angry with me. She thinks I lied to her. You said the baby wasn't mine."

"Andrew, I didn't think he was, but I couldn't be positive until he was born—ten months after we were together. He's not yours."

"I don't believe you. If he's mine, I have a right to shared custody."

"Leave, Andrew."

"I'm going to see an attorney."

"For your own sake, you shouldn't do that, but if you do, I'll deal with it. Now leave."

"Jo, if he isn't mine, whose is he? How can he look that much like Adam? Like me? If he isn't mine, why didn't you tell me six years ago whose he was?"

"You wouldn't have believed me. Andrew, I was never unfaithful to you. For a time, I did wonder if getting pregnant with Tanner was punishment for what we did, which we both considered wrong. In time, I came to accept that he wasn't a punishment, but our being together did complicate things."

"I don't understand. If he's not mine…. If you weren't unfaithful…."

"Andrew, I was raped. One month after we were together. Nine months before Tanner was born."

Andrew staggered and tears came to his eyes. "No." He wiped at the tears with both hands. "Jo, if I had known, we would have married, and we would have raised Tanner as if he were my own. We could have kept the secret together, been together." He shook his head. "But I never gave you a chance to tell me, did I?"

"No, you didn't. I'm not sure it would have mattered. I could never tell you who raped me. It was someone…close to you…and it would have always been there between us every time you touched me. We both deserved better than that."

"Someone close to me? One of my brothers or cousins? It had to be for Tanner and Adam to be so much alike. I am sorry, Jo. If Tracey and I weren't married—"

"But you are. And I'm glad you are. Not at first. My heart ached when Paige told me you had married. But I knew we could never be together, and I was thankful that you had a wife and hopefully could have as many children as you wanted."

"Can you have other children? Did you have problems when you were pregnant with Tanner like the doctor feared?"

"I did. Ironically, if you hadn't comforted me that night after my diagnosis, we would never have been together, but we also wouldn't be having this conversation now."

"You were distraught. You wanted children. I wanted children. But that doctor advised you not to have children."

"I was distraught. All I had ever wanted was to have a husband, a home, and children."

"I only wanted to comfort you."

"I know, and one thing led to another. If you hadn't carried protection…."

"That was my dad's idea. He said sometimes things happen that you don't mean to happen. I never thought it would, and then it did. But it was only that one time, and I did use the protection. Still, I always wondered."

"I wondered, too, at first. I was naïve but not enough to not know protection can fail. And I did think for a selfish moment that if he were yours, you would never have to know about the rape. But I would know, and the rapist would wonder. I couldn't live with the doubt and worry. And I couldn't live in our small town where I might see him any day, anywhere."

"And you knew that I never wanted to leave our hometown. So…how do you know for sure?"

"Besides the timing? Remember the hairbrush you left at my house?"

"Yes, I always wondered what happened to that hairbrush."

"I took it with me. When I took it, it was only because it was something to remind me of you. Like my engagement ring. Which, by the way, I had to sell to support Tanner and me after he was born because I had to have a C-section and couldn't work for two months."

"I'm glad you had it with you, then. And the hairbrush?"

"After Tanner was born, I took hairs from the hairbrush and a saliva sample from Tanner and had them tested. You are not his father."

"But you aren't going to tell me who is?"

"No."

"But our life together. Your life…."

"My life might have been better with you, but yours might not have been. We were both disappointed when we learned that I might not be able to bring a child to term. We could have adopted, but then, of course, there was my dysfunctional family. I would no doubt have been dysfunctional in our family as well. I didn't know we were dysfunctional at the time. I would have never thought to see a therapist if I hadn't gone through what I did."

"You did see one then?"

"Yes, and in some ways, it has helped. A lot. In other ways, I'm still working on healing."

"I'm sorry, Jo. I wish I could do more than say empty words. I'm sorry I blew up like I did when I thought you had lied to me. Had been unfaithful to me. What will you do? Will you tell your parents the truth? Will you tell them who the father is?"

"They wouldn't have believed me then. I'm not convinced they would believe me now. And I won't have Tanner brought up in such a state as might exist if I did tell them. I'm not sure my parents could ever love him. He's my son and the light of my life. I love him, and I will not allow his childhood to be marred by that knowledge or that treatment."

"Not everyone could have done what you did."

"I know that. At first, I didn't think I could. I planned, if I managed to carry him to full term, to give him up for adoption. But when I held that perfect, pure, innocent baby in my arms, I knew I couldn't. He might not have been conceived in love, but at least he could be brought up in love. My love."

"Does Tanner know who his father is?"

"Of course not. I told him his father died. I didn't want him to be traumatized by the details of his birth. It was enough that

I was. At some point, after he's an adult, I will tell him, but not now."

"And there's nothing I can do to persuade you to tell me who stole you away from me."

"No one stole me away from you. I never stopped loving you."

"Then why did you leave?"

"Why? After my parents kicked me out? After you walked away from me? Why would I stay? Besides, it was best…for both of us…for all of us."

"All of us? What do you mean?"

"I…. Never mind. It doesn't matter now."

"Jo, I never stopped loving you either. I was hurt, heartbroken, but I never stopped loving you. I…I even thought you might give the baby up for adoption and come back home. Your parents thought you would abort the baby, but I knew you would never do that. I waited a year before I ever dated anyone else. After that year, I gave up. Even now, I'm tempted…."

"Andrew, stop. We could never be together. Not then and not now. Not ever. I am glad we had this talk, but now you need to go. Don't come to Paige's again. And as much as I would hate to do so, if Tracey accosts us again, especially when Tanner is with me, I will take out a restraining order on both of you. Now, please leave."

Andrew swallowed a sob. "You take care of yourself. And of Tanner."

"I will. You do the same."

Andrew nodded and left.

Jo watched him as he walked head down to his car where Tracey sat with their children. The little boy had his head against the back glass. She could not deny that Adam, though younger, did look like Tanner's mirror image. Only she knew why. After they pulled away, she went back inside where everyone waited for her. She smiled and reached out for Tanner. He jumped into her arms, and she carried him to the Kia as Paige and Roger carried Michael and Tabitha to their SUV. She was thankful she and Paige had decided not to go to

Sunday School but to church services only, thankful that Andrew and his wife attended Tracey's childhood church and not his. She only hoped she did not run into Andrew's parents.

* * *

After leaving the children at children's church, Jo, Paige, and Roger took seats at the back of the church auditorium. Jo kept her head down throughout the service though she doubted anyone would notice or recognize her. After the benediction, she and Paige rushed out and downstairs to the Sunday School room where the children's church was held. When Tanner saw her, he ran to her and jumped into her arms while waving the picture he had colored that morning.

"Mommy, Mommy, see my picture? I colored inside the lines!"

"I see!" she said. "Yes, you did. I'm proud of you." She kissed his cheek and turned to leave.

Blocking the way were several of the younger ladies of the church, former classmates of Jo and Paige, who stood at the door waiting to collect their own children.

"Well, well," said one of the women. "This is just like one of those TV shows where the prodigal child returns home."

Jo stared at them as they eyed her with disdain and Tanner with curiosity.

"My, my," said another one of the women. "He looks just like—"

"He looks just like himself," said Jo cutting the woman off. Then she raced up the stairs and out of the church where she skidded to a stop. Gwen and Beth stood facing the church a few feet in front of her. Both threw their hands over their mouths. Jo dashed to her Kia, struggled to fasten Tanner into his booster seat, jumped in front, and spun her tires leaving the church parking lot.

She blinked back tears and checked Tanner through the rearview mirror. He looked terrified.

"Tanner, everything is okay. We're on our way to Paige's house. Mommy just got in a little bit of a hurry."

"Can we go back to church tonight?"

"No, honey, I don't think so. Mommy needs to rest."

"I could go with Auntie Paige."

"No, not tonight. Maybe Michael and Tabitha will stay at home with you."

"I hope so."

"Me, too."

What was I thinking? Jo shook her head. *I was thinking my only concerns were Andrew and Tracey and Andrew's parents. I was thinking no one would know Paige's visitors were me and my son. I was thinking I could get in and out without Mom or Beth seeing us. How stupid. Stupid. Stupid. Well, I planned to tell them tomorrow. I can't change my mind now.*

CHAPTER EIGHT

Monday, June 14, 2021

Monday morning came too soon for Jo. She dreaded confronting her parents with the events surrounding Tanner's conception and birth. Would they even allow her to tell her story? They had refused to listen six years ago.

She sat on the side of the bed, dressed and ready to leave. She had overslept, and she and Tanner had eaten breakfast with Paige's family in their pajamas. Paige had offered to dress Tanner later when she dressed Michael and Tabitha. The three were downstairs watching cartoons at the moment.

"I have to leave. Now." She spoke to the empty room, her eyes focused on nothing. "I have to tell them. I'm here. It's past time to do this. Mom has already seen Tanner. I can imagine what she thinks. If she's told Dad, he will think the same thing. But I still cannot tell them who Tanner's biological father is. I cannot. Especially not after Dad's stroke. I cannot set him up for a second one." She closed her eyes. "Guide me, Lord. Give me the words to say, and prepare my parents to hear what I tell them. Help them to accept it without Dad having another stroke, without Mom having a breakdown of any kind."

A knock on the door brought her to her feet.

"Yes?"

"It's Paige. Are you decent? Can I get Tanner's clothes?"

"I am. You can. Come on in."

Paige peeped around the door. "Tanner wants a hug before you leave." He peeped around Paige.

Jo grinned and stood. "Come on in you two. Come here, sweet boy." He ran to her, and she lifted him and swung him around before hugging him close. "Are you going to be a good boy for Paige today?"

"I am."

"Good. What do you two say to a couple of large pizzas for tonight?"

"Yay! Pizza! Enough for Michael and Tabitha, too?"

"You bet! And Auntie Paige and Uncle Roger and Mommy, too!"

"We need colas, Mommy."

"Yes, we do. I'll take care of that, too. Now give Mommy a kiss, get dressed, and go play! I'll see you tonight."

Tanner kissed her and wiggled out of her arms. He grabbed Paige by the hand and dragged her to where his clothes were. "Come on Auntie Paige. Time's wastin'!"

"What?" asked Jo.

"Time is a-wasting. That's Roger's favorite phrase to get the kids moving. Apparently, his grandmother said that to him at least twice every day of his childhood."

"I like it. Paige, has Roger left yet?"

"No. Why?"

"Could he stay with the kids long enough for you to carry me to Art and Gwen's house? I need to discuss something with you."

"Sure."

"Tanner, will you let Roger dress you?"

"Of course. He helps dress Michael."

"Good. See you later!"

"Later, Mommy!"

On the drive over, Jo told Paige what she planned to tell and not to tell her parents that morning.

"What do you think?"

"I agree with you one hundred percent. You have no choice about what you plan to tell them. And you should wait about what you do not plan to tell them. That might need a little more thought."

"Agreed."

As Jo unbuckled her seat belt, Paige reached over to give her a hug. "Good luck, dear."

"Thanks, I may need that and more."

* * *

Jo's parents were waiting for her in the living room, but Art had already turned off the TV. His face was red. Gwen sat on the sofa twisting a tissue to shreds.

"Mom. Dad. Are you both all right?"

"I told him, Jo. I told him I saw your son. And I told him he looked like Andrew's boy, Adam. Is he Andrew's?"

"You told us Andrew was not the father. Why would you tell us that? Why wouldn't Andrew tell us the truth? Tell his parents the truth?"

Once again, Jo dropped into the armchair near the doorway and then dropped her bags onto the floor, all the while conscious of her mom and dad staring at her, waiting for her to speak. To tell them the truth.

"Mom, Dad. Andrew was not, is not, Tanner's father. I swear to you he is not. I know Tanner favors Adam, but he is not Andrew's son."

"Then whose is he?" yelled Art. "Who else were you seeing while you were engaged to marry Andrew?"

"I wasn't seeing anyone else, Dad. I…." She bit her lip and blinked back her tears. "Dad. Mom. I was raped."

Art tried to force himself out of his chair but fell back breathless. Gwen sounded like she was going to hyperventilate. She clutched at Art's arm, and he grabbed her hand with his.

"Catch your breath, Gwen. Take a few deep ones and calm down. Jo, if that's true, why wouldn't you tell us? We're your parents. I would have killed the…I would have killed him."

"Why wouldn't I tell you? Why would I? It wasn't the truth that mattered. I was your daughter. You abandoned me in a moment because you thought I had sinned, because I had fallen short of your expectations, your ideals. I was your daughter, and I had disappointed you, and instead of forgiving me for what you thought I had done, instead of supporting me, you forsook me altogether. That hurt my heart as much as his actions hurt my body. As for you killing my rapist, I was afraid you might try or even succeed. And you could have ended up in prison. But the real truth is that you didn't give me a chance to tell you. We never talked about serious things. You'd get upset or angry. Mom would have a spell. You would both tell Beth and me to pray about whatever it was, and God would take care of it. But that's what He put you here for, Dad. You and Mom. To take care of Beth and me. And sometimes…sometimes…He expects us to take care of things ourselves. But we can't always do that if we don't know how. And we never discussed the how of things. And…and I had to go through almost losing Tanner alone."

Gwen swallowed hard. "What do you mean, you almost lost Tanner. What happened?"

"Oh, Mom. I had a medical problem. I wish I had told you about it, but I was afraid you wouldn't understand. About my problem or about my reaction to it."

"What problem?"

"A problem I learned about just after I turned eighteen but one I had been dealing with since I was thirteen."

"I don't understand. How did you figure out that whatever it was began when you were thirteen?"

"My therapist—"

"Your therapist? You've been in therapy?"

"Yes, Mom. For about three years now. She asked me if certain…things in life…had started before I was raped. I thought about it, and I realized they had."

"I still don't understand. Did your father and I do something?"

"It wasn't so much that you did anything but rather that you didn't understand much less know how to help."

"Humph." Art twisted in his wheelchair. "Therapists always blame it on the parents. We didn't do anything."

"Hush, Art. Let Jo finish."

A look of surprise crossed all three of their faces. Jo's mom had never spoken or acted contrary to her father.

"You heard your mother. Go on. Finish."

"It was just before I turned thirteen that my hormones kicked in. My stress and teenage angst stressed both of you as well as Beth. By the time I turned fourteen, my temper tantrums, my stubborn streak, and my rebelliousness were in full force. Mom, you tried to defend me, telling Dad you were convinced it was just teenage growing pains. Dad said he didn't care what the reason was, and my behavior only served to trigger his temper more than ever.

"As my cycles had always been irregular, right after I turned eighteen, I decided to ask my doctor about it. I don't know why I didn't ask him before then—or why you didn't ask him. If I had connected my emotional states with my periods—and my hormones—I might have, but I didn't. His diagnosis was the final blow to my psyche. He said I had PCOS—polycystic ovary syndrome. He said I might have trouble getting pregnant. If I did, I could easily miscarry. Even if I didn't, complications could threaten both the baby's life and my life. He discouraged me from ever trying to get pregnant. I was heartbroken that I might never be able to have a family, and I was terrified that if I did, the baby or I or both of us would die."

"How did we not realize this?"

"Maybe partly because I was such an active child. If I hadn't been, I could have had weight problems, and you would have worried about that. Even now, I stay active to ward off diabetes and heart problems both of which can be related to PCOS."

"Why didn't you tell us?" asked Gwen.

"Truth?" Her mother nodded. "I never told you about the PCOS or about my fears because I knew what your responses would be. You would have dismissed my concerns and told me to trust the Lord. Even if I could have handled your telling me to trust the Lord, I couldn't handle you dismissing my concerns. All I had ever really wanted was to have my own home, a husband I loved and who loved me, and a houseful of children. Alone in my anguish, how could I trust the Lord when all I wanted to do was question Him?"

"But you had Tanner," said Art. "He's alive and healthy. Wasn't that proof of the Lord's hand?"

"Art, she said she almost lost Tanner. Jo, what happened?"

"Fortunately, I was scared enough that as soon as I got settled after leaving home, I saw an OB/GYN. She was knowledgeable and helpful, but I did have complications when Tanner was born, and I did have to have a C-section. I'm doing well now. I maintain a healthy diet and exercise program and take appropriate medications. I do worry about having another child but not as much as I would have if I'd lost Tanner. Which I might have done if I hadn't stayed with my OB/GYN. I almost didn't go back to her after my first visit because after pointing out the potential problems, she told me I could have an abortion."

"No. She shouldn't have done that."

"No, and I told her so. I guess I gave her one of Dad's glares because she drew back and said, 'What?' I kept glaring and said, 'I thought that was supposed to be my choice.' She said, 'It is, but—' I interrupted her and said, 'Then I've made my choice.' She looked at me somewhat incredulously and said, 'Even if you die or the baby dies?' When I said, 'Yes,' she stared at me for a moment and then said, 'Then we'll do the best we can. However, at the first sign of trouble, I want to see you every week, sooner if you feel the need.' And that's what we did. And that's how we knew Tanner was in trouble soon enough to save him by taking him. And that's why if I ever have another child, she will be my doctor."

"My little girl. All alone. I'm sorry I wasn't there for you. I'm sorry we didn't listen to you before you left."

"I didn't actually leave. I was driven off." Jo glanced at her father. He had turned away from her, but she could see his lips trembling. "Dad?"

"What's done is done. It's in the past. We can't go back and change it now."

"No, we can't. But we can change the future."

He turned to face her. Tears clouded his eyes. "I hope so."

A knock at the door interrupted them.

"That would be your therapist, Dad. As you told Mom, take a deep breath and calm yourself. You need the therapy, and Mom and I do not need you to have another stroke."

Art nodded once. Gwen went to the door and brought the therapist back with her.

* * *

The rest of that day was busy with therapy and home health and naps in between. Jo didn't have another chance to continue their earlier discussion, but she did overhear her mother on the phone with Beth repeating everything they had said that morning almost word-for-word.

That evening, Beth delighted Jo by having her husband Alex and her daughter Maddie accompany her.

When they walked into the living room, three-year-old Maddie pointed and said, "That Aunt Jo?"

"Yes," said Beth, "that's Aunt Jo."

Jo pressed her lips together and wiped at the tears that threatened to break through.

"Hello, Maddie. It's nice to meet you. You're even prettier in person than you are in your pictures."

Maddie reached out to Jo, and Jo took her. The child hugged her and patted her face.

"You pretty, too." Maddie jumped at the sound of a knock on the door. "Got company!"

"It sounds like it," said Jo.

"I'll get it," said Beth.

"Hug Grandpa and Grandma now," said Maddie as she wiggled out of Jo's arms and into her grandmother's.

Jo watched them and smiled—until she heard the voices of Andrew's parents at the door. She frowned and glanced at her father. He was smiling at Maddie as she climbed down from her grandmother's lap and up into his. Jo swallowed and crossed the room to sit beside her mother.

Peggy Richards spoke first. "We came to visit our little Maddie. We saw her get out of the car with Beth and Alex."

"There's our Maddie," said Frank Richards with a grin. The grin faded when he saw Jo. "And there's our prodigal Josephine."

"Jo," said Peggy, "we didn't think you were here today. Where did you park your car?"

"Paige brought me this morning. We had some things to discuss. She'll be picking me up any minute now. I need to gather my things." She popped off the sofa and went upstairs to grab her bags from her old bedroom. She froze at the bottom of the stairs when she returned and saw the look in Frank's eyes as he watched Maddie.

"Come see Uncle Frank, Maddie."

Jo bit her lip as Maddie pouted and shook her head.

"No. See Grandpa."

Jo's cell phone chirped with a message from Paige. *Outside. Have kids. Will wait here.*

"Mom, Dad, Paige is here. I'll be back tomorrow. Beth, walk me to the door." At the door, she whispered to Beth, "Do not let them babysit Maddie."

"Why?" asked Beth. "Does this have anything to do with Tanner? Mom told me, you know."

"I know. I heard her. We'll talk later. But for now, just don't leave Maddie with them. Please. But don't mention anything to Mom and Dad." Then she rushed out the door. She was trembling when she got into the SUV.

* * *

After putting Tanner to bed that night, Jo shared her fears with Paige. They agreed that she had to follow through with her plans to confront Tanner's father—the one thing she dreaded more than anything else.

As she got ready for bed, her cell phone chirped. It was Noah.

"Noah, I was hoping you would call tonight."

"Because you couldn't wait to hear my voice or something else?"

"Both actually."

"I'm glad for the first. I miss you, Jo."

"I miss you, too." Jo waited for a response. She heard only silence. "Are you there?"

"I am. You caught me by surprise. I didn't expect you to respond in kind."

"I know. Noah, I really do care about you, and I'm sorry I've been slow to show it, but I knew I had to face my past—and those in it—before I could tell you about it. And I had to tell you before we could go forward—if we can."

"Nothing will prevent that for me, Jo."

"I hope not, but I have to be sure."

"You plan to deal with whatever this is while you're home?"

"I do."

"When? How? Who?"

"I've already dealt with all but one person. My parents, my sister, and my old boyfriend now know almost everything. That has been progressive if not always positive. Thus far, I haven't been able to tell them the final piece. After tonight, I know I have to tell them that, too. Before I do, though, I have to confront Tanner's birthfather."

"I thought that might be the one last person. That means your old boyfriend is not Tanner's father."

"No, he isn't."

"Does the father know he's Tanner's father?"

"No, although he may suspect it. Noah, he…. Noah, over the telephone is not how I meant to do this. But after tonight, I don't think I can wait until I get back to Nashville."

"Tell me."

"Noah, six years ago before I left home, I…I was raped."

"Jo. I am sorry. You don't need to face him alone. I'm coming to you."

"No. Not yet. Maybe afterwards. I'll tell you when."

"Neither your parents nor your old boyfriend knew this when you left home."

"No."

"Did they know you were pregnant?"

"They did."

"How did they react?"

"Not well at all."

"That's why you left, and that's why you didn't tell them the rest."

"Yes."

"Jo, I'm going to reschedule my upcoming surgeries, and I'm coming to you."

"Noah—"

"No arguments. Please. I want to be there for you."

Neither of them said anything for several heartbeats.

"Jo?"

"Will you let me know when you leave Nashville?"

"I will."

"I have to go before I break down and cry. I'll talk to you later. Good night, Noah."

"Good night, Jo."

Jo disconnected the call and slid to the floor. Tears flooded her eyes. Sobs racked her body. When she finally regained control, she shook her head and whispered to herself. "I don't know if I'm crying for fear, for relief, or for the last six years. Whatever it is, there will be no more secrets after tomorrow."

As she climbed into bed and closed her eyes, her brain began to rerun the events of that other night two months before she left home.

CHAPTER NINE

Wednesday, April 15, 2015

Jo had spent the evening at Paige's house and had walked home. It was still light enough to see, and she had walked home from Paige's a million times over the years.

When they were younger, Paige's father would walk Jo home and Jo's father would walk Paige home. When they were older, they walked home by themselves. They lived in a quiet, safe neighborhood. Perhaps they had been naïve, both the girls and their parents. Who could have known how close the danger really was?

When she arrived at her house, she saw that the inside lights were out, which could only mean that neither her parents nor her sister were at home. That was not a problem. She had her own key.

As she walked up to her front porch, Frank Richards, Andrew's father, called to her. "Your parents aren't home. They said for you to come stay with us. Peggy sent me to tell you to come watch a movie with us."

Jo hesitated. "I'm eighteen years old. I don't need a babysitter."

"I know, but your father will be angry with all three of us if we don't follow his instructions."

She knew he was right. Besides, she and her sister Beth had been doing this all their lives. The Richards had babysat them since they were infants. Even when they got older, it was a given that if their parents were not home, she and Beth should wait for them with the Richards. And he said Peggy sent him to tell her. As long as Peggy was in the house, everything would be all right.

When Jo entered the Richards' home, the house was silent. No movie played on the TV in the living room.

She heard the lock on the front door click. But that was not unusual. Both families always locked their doors.

She called out to Peggy, but she didn't answer. She called out to Andrew, but he didn't answer, either.

Before she could turn to question Frank, he grabbed her from behind, gripping her in a vise she could not break. She felt the terror rise in her chest.

"Frank, what are you doing?"

"I've waited your whole life for this," he said. "I've watched you become the woman you are. I loved you long before Andrew did, and I've never been thrilled about the engagement."

"I have to leave."

"No, you don't. Not yet."

She fought him as he carried her up the stairs, but she had no self-defense skills, and he was twice her size and stronger. He had grown up on a dairy farm accustomed to wrestling calves to the ground. She was no match for him. Still she fought—even after he threw her on the bed in his and Peggy's bedroom—until he swung at her and knocked her out.

She came to struggling against him. And then it was over.

As he lifted himself off the bed, he said, "I need a beer. I'll be back."

For a moment, she was stunned. By what had happened. But also by Frank leaving her there to get a beer. She had never known him to drink any form of alcohol. She hadn't even known they kept it in the house. What else had she not known about Andrew's parents?

But as soon as he left the room, she shook herself out of her stupor, jerked her clothes on, and stumbled down the stairs. As she unlocked the front door, she heard him calling.

"Come back here. Come back here!"

She didn't stop. She raced down the porch steps and across both lawns. Her hands shook as she dug the key to her house out of her jeans pocket and tried to unlock the door. The lock clicked as he started up the porch steps behind her. She darted inside the house, slammed the door shut, and locked it just as he reached it. He banged on it and yelled at her to let him in. She dragged herself up the stairs to her own bedroom and locked that door. Then she ran into her bathroom and locked that door as well.

When she could no longer hear Frank banging on the outside door, she stripped off her clothes and tied them together in a trash bag. She would burn then tomorrow. Then she jumped into the shower and scrubbed until her skin felt raw and the water flowed cold. She shivered as she pulled on a sweatsuit and tiptoed to her closet where she hid until she heard her parents come home later that night. Then she unlocked the door to her bedroom, jumped into her bed, and pulled the covers up around her neck.

She knew her mother would check on her. If she could just feign sleep, she could get through the night. Her mother did check on her and did assume she was asleep.

But she wasn't. She cried until she had no tears left, and still she cried. How could she tell her parents? Andrew? His mother? Would they even believe her? What could she say or do? How could she say or do anything? The telling of it would destroy both families. If they believed her. Her word against that of an upstanding deacon in the church. As she sobbed silently into her pillow, she vowed that no one would ever overpower her again. She would enroll in a self-defense class the next day, and she would never stop training.

She finally fell asleep sometime in the early morning hours. Only later did she learn that Peggy had gone with her parents and Beth to the movies, and Andrew had gone out with some of his buddies.

CHAPTER TEN

Tuesday, June 15, 2021

Jo had slept fitfully the night before, plagued in her dreams by the events of that summer six years ago. She got out of bed long before anyone else was awake, determined to leave early and confront her tormentor first thing.

She breakfasted on a single piece of dry toast and a cup of coffee and was ready to leave by the time the others were awake. After hugs around and a quick "Don't worry" to Paige, she left.

She parked her car in her parents' driveway and walked across both yards to the Richards' front door. She lowered her head, uttered a silent prayer, and rang the doorbell. She looked up as it opened.

"Well," said Frank, "look what the cat dragged in. I didn't think you would condescend to visit us. Peggy's in the shower."

"I didn't come to see Peggy," said Jo. "I came to speak my piece and to warn you."

"Then by all means, come in."

Frank led the way into the living room and sat in his recliner. Jo stood in front of the sofa.

"Have a seat," said Frank.

"I'll stand," said Jo.

"Suit yourself. You're welcome to say what you need to say, but let me say this first. You think you were special? You think—"

"I trusted you. I loved you and Peggy like second parents."

"I know you did. I worked hard for that trust and that love. But as I was about to say, you weren't the first, and you won't be the last."

Jo shook her head, stunned by his confession. She couldn't let that stop her from what she needed to say, but his words brought up new questions.

"There were others? Did Peggy know? Did Andrew or his brothers know? Did…did my father know?"

"Peggy has always had her head in the sand. She's a dutiful, obedient wife, just like your mother. His brothers? I'm not sure about them. For the most part, I think they were clueless. Andrew? I always thought Andrew suspected something, but I never knew what, and he never challenged me. As for your father? He always thought he was Mr. Goodie Two Shoes, but he wasn't a saint, was he? Not with that temper of his. But no, he was clueless about my little extracurricular activities. He would have balked at that. Now. It's your turn."

"Do you have no shame? Feel no remorse?"

"Not in the least."

"Frank, you and Dad taught us kids right from wrong. Taught us the Word of God. Did you believe any of it?"

He shrugged. "Some of it."

"I always looked up to both of you and Mom and Peggy. Even after what you did, I tried to live by the words you and Dad preached—and professed to live by—'Forgive that you might be forgiven.' No longer because you said them but because the words you professed were the words of God. It was the hardest thing I have ever done, but I have forgiven you, and you no longer have a hold on me or my future. That said, Frank Richards, forgiveness does not excuse what you did. It does not take away the damage you did or prevent the consequences, and it does not release you from your responsibility or cleanse your heart. You raped me. You stole my life from me. You scorned the very God you professed to believe in. I cannot forget what you did. I cannot forgive you for God. Only He can do that. Only he can redeem your soul."

Frank stared at her for a moment before responding. "Right. And the warning?"

"Do you have no conscience left? Whether or no, your sin against my family ends with me. You and Peggy will never babysit Maddie or any siblings she may have ever again. You will also resign any positions you hold in the church, including as a deacon and as a Sunday School teacher effective immediately. If you do not, I will bring it before the deacon body myself. And if you ever lay a hand on Maddie or any future children Beth and Alex may have or any other children or any other young women, I will forget protecting our families from the broken heartedness of our community knowing the truth. I will protect the children whatever it takes, and that includes Tanner. I will not stand by and watch it happen again."

"Speaking of Tanner. I would like to see my son. I have a right to see him. However, I do hope you won't tell your parents who his father is. You could push Art into another stroke, even a massive one. You wouldn't want that on your conscience, would you?"

"My conscience? As for Dad, you aren't worried about him having a stroke. You're only worried about what he might do. You know what he would want to do. He would want to kill you with his bare hands."

"He might want to, but he isn't—never was—able to do that."

"You hope he isn't. As for being Tanner's father, what you did does not make you or any man a father. He is not your son in any sense of the word. You may not ever see or contact him. If you try, I will bring charges against you."

"You were eighteen, and you never reported it. You've waited too long to bring charges."

"Too long to bring charges against you for rape? No, I haven't. I still have a couple of years before the statute of limitations runs out."

"You have no proof. It would be my word against yours."

"I may not have proof that would stand up in a court of law. But Tanner is proof enough to stand up in the court of public opinion. I can tell the world what you did. Furthermore, I can charge you with threatening the life of my son."

Art smirked. "You don't honestly think anyone would believe you, do you?"

"They might not believe me at all if I hadn't gotten pregnant. But as I said, Tanner is proof enough. You should have practiced what you preached to Andrew about protection."

"I could say Tanner was Andrew's son."

"You would do that to your own son? You really are a despicable man. But it wouldn't work anyway. His children, your grandchildren, would share only about twenty-five percent of your DNA. Your children would share about fifty percent. Even as half-siblings, Andrew and Tanner would still share about fifty percent. And guess what? I've done the sibling tests. Andrew and Tanner both share fifty percent of your DNA. They are half-brothers. You've been warned, Frank Richards. Stay away from Tanner. Stay away from Maddie. As for my telling the world, that will depend on you. As for telling my family—and Andrew—that I will do. Prepare yourself." Jo turned and stomped out of the house, slamming the door behind her.

CHAPTER ELEVEN

Jo forced herself to appear calm when she entered her parents' house. In spite of the turmoil inside her, she went about her parents' routine with them being none the wiser.

At noon, Noah called to tell her he had rescheduled his surgeries, all of which had been elective, for the next two days and would be leaving Nashville at four o'clock that evening. He expected to arrive at Paige's house a little after six o'clock.

"Don't speed," said Jo. "Be careful. I don't need another patient on my hands."

"I won't speed. When will you leave your parents' house?"

"Between seven and seven-thirty, depending on when Beth arrives. If it's not too late, you and I could come back a little later for you to meet my parents and them to meet you. I want us to talk first, though."

"I'm yours to command. Does Paige know I'm coming? Should I get a hotel room?"

"She knows, and she'll have the second guest bedroom ready for you."

"They must have a big house."

"They do. Noah, I'm glad you're coming."

"I am, too. Now let me get off the phone and finish up here so I can leave on time. I'll see you this evening."

"I'll be waiting." Jo disconnected. She jumped as her mother came into the kitchen.

"Who was that, dear?"

"A friend. A good friend."

Jo decided to wait about telling her parents about Noah until that night when she brought him to meet them. After a moment's thought, she called Beth to ask her if she could come at six instead of seven. She explained to her briefly that the man she had been seeing was coming from Nashville, and she wanted to meet him and talk to him before bringing him to meet their parents. She cautioned Beth not to mention it to Art and Gwen. For once, Beth agreed without questioning her.

Then Jo called Noah back and asked him to meet her at the nearby park so they could talk before they went to her parents' house. She would pick up burgers on her way.

* * *

Jo arrived at the park shortly before Noah did. She chose a picnic table that sat away from the others. When she saw him get out of his Lexus, she wanted to run to him. She waited as long as she could and met him halfway. They wrapped their arms around each other and held each other close for several moments—until the rumbling in Jo's stomach reminded them that they were hungry for food as well as affection.

As they ate, Jo told Noah her story from beginning to end starting with the changes that began when she was thirteen. Her diagnosis with PCOS. Hers and Andrew's relationship, their one sexual encounter, and their guilt over that. The night she was raped. Discovering that she was pregnant. Her turmoil over telling their families the whole truth. Being kicked out of her parents' house. Almost losing Tanner. Her decision to keep him. Her struggle to go to school, work part time, and care for her son. And meeting Noah.

"I was drawn to you from the first time we met," she told him as she took his hand in hers. "But I was scared. Scared of being hurt again. Scared of what you would think of me for my not telling anyone what happened. Especially given the *Me Too* movement which hit full force by the middle of the first semester of my junior year at Vanderbilt. If I'd known about it when I was eighteen, maybe I wouldn't have been too terrified to speak out. But I didn't, and I was. Even after all those women did speak out, I was still too scared. I'd kept my baby. I couldn't expose him to all of that. I continued to hold it in. Struggled to hold myself—my life—together.

"Then in the middle of the spring semester of my junior year, I took a creative writing class. One of the women in the class shared a poem about her own experiences that both upset me and inspired me. It was also because of that class that I began journaling. The poem and my journaling led me to compare my own life to that of the woman who wrote the poem. If no one had believed her about a word and a touch, how could I have expected anyone to believe my story? If she had experienced what she had from a touch and words, no wonder I had experienced what I had. Even if no one had believed me, my story would have destroyed both families.

"I realized I needed help to come to terms with all that had—or had not—happened. That led me, at the end of that semester, to begin seeing Dr. Weber and opening up about my past. To her. Still not to anyone else. In time, she suggested that at some point, for my own peace of mind, I might need to face the past in reality, not just in my mind and my heart. I got that, but I wondered how or even if I could do it.

"And then Beth called. I still didn't know how or if, but I thought maybe this was the time. Even if it was, I would have to tread softly because of my dad's health. Softly hasn't worked that well, but I have confronted them all." She gave him a brief account of each of those confrontations and their responses as well as the verbal attacks by others during the few days she had been home. "But…I still haven't told my parents, my sister, or Andrew who raped me."

"Jo, if Tanner looks so much like Andrew and his son, was it a brother or a cousin?"

"No."

Neither of them spoke for what seemed like an eternity.

"It was…." Jo sucked in air.

Noah clenched his teeth and pounded the table with his fists. "His father."

"Yes." Jo burst into tears.

Noah rushed to Jo's side and pulled her close. "I'm so sorry, Jo. I can't imagine the betrayal you must have felt. I don't know how you managed—not just to get through it—but to accomplish all that you did. You're a strong woman."

Jo pulled back enough to look into Noah's eyes. "I don't know about strong. I struggled. Being busy helped me to not think about it during the daytime. But every night after Tanner fell asleep and I finished my classwork, I fell apart and cried myself to sleep. That went on until I started seeing Dr. Weber."

"She's a good therapist."

"She is. I resisted at first, but she was patient, and by the time I entered my graduate program, I felt like I'd moved beyond it, I guess. But of course, I hadn't. Not completely. If I had, I wouldn't have held you at arm's length. Dr. Weber was right. I needed them to know, to understand."

Noah stroked Jo's hair back from her face. He tilted her chin and leaned in to kiss her. Jo didn't pull away. The kiss was short and gentle, but to Jo, it felt like the end of one life and the beginning of another.

"Jo, I would never have rejected you or thought less of you for any of those reasons. You are in no way responsible for what happened to you. Neither is Tanner. I love you both."

"Thank you for saying that. I couldn't even consider a real relationship with you—or the possibility of you leaving us— until I could tell you everything. And I couldn't tell you until I faced all those in the past myself. And Noah…I love you, too. I was just afraid to admit it even to myself."

"I'm not going to leave you and Tanner. As for future children, if at some point, you—or we—want other children, adoption is always an option. That said, if you—we—wanted a biological child, and you were afraid to go through that again, you do have another option. You could have a surrogate. Please, don't limit yourself and don't push me away for any reason."

Noah leaned in for another kiss, one that lasted a little longer and left Jo breathless.

When they pulled away the second time, she placed a hand on his chest. "I won't ever limit myself again. And I'll never push you away. I'd like for you to meet my parents now."

"I'd like that, too."

CHAPTER TWELVE

Jo texted Beth to tell her that she and Noah were on their way. Beth met them at the front door.

Jo froze when she heard the voices from the living room. "What is he doing here?" she spit out in a whisper.

Beth stepped outside and eased the door closed behind her. "That's why I met you. I've been watching for you. I've been ready to scream, but I didn't know what to do. He and Peggy knocked on the door right after you texted me that you were on your way. Andrew showed up a few minutes later. I don't know what's going on, but Frank told Mom and Dad that he and Peggy had come over to commiserate with them about their *wayward daughter*. He said he didn't mean to make it a big to-do, but Peggy insisted on coming with him, and he had no idea why Andrew had showed up. He keeps saying things that make it sound like you were always a liar, and they just didn't know it. We were all just sitting there, listening to him, stunned. What's he trying to pull?"

"Beth, do Mom and Dad seem to be believing him?"

"Not Mom. She keeps shaking her head and whispering, 'Not Jo. Not Jo.' Dad looks angry, but I don't know if he's angry with you because he believes it or if he's angry with Frank for saying it. Peggy keeps saying, 'Frank, you know that's not true.' And Andrew. He looks like he's about to explode. As I left to open the door, he said, 'Dad, what are you trying to do?' Jo, you need to get in there. I don't know what's happening, but I don't like it."

As Jo pushed the door open and led Beth and Noah inside, she said, "I do know, and I don't like it either." Once in the living room, she stood, feet apart and hands on her hips, glaring at Frank. "What do you think you're doing, Frank Richards?"

He sneered at her and said, "Telling the truth."

"That's a lie, and you know it."

Peggy, sitting on the opposite side of the room, stood up and took a step forward. "Thank goodness you're here, Jo. I know what he's saying isn't true. That's why I insisted on coming with him. But I didn't know what to do to stop him." She looked fearfully at her husband. "Jo, I heard you and Frank this morning. I had just come out of the shower when you arrived. I heard that whole terrible conversation. I've been beside myself all day, but I didn't know what to do. When he said he was coming over here to tell Art about what an awful daughter you had been, I panicked." She glanced at her husband again. "That's why I called Andrew and insisted he meet us here."

Jo looked at Andrew. His confusion and anger were written all over his face.

"Peggy, did you tell Andrew what you heard?"

"No, I was afraid to." She stepped across the room to stand beside her son.

"Jo," said her father, "what's this about? What terrible thing did you have to talk to Frank about?"

Jo was certain by the look on her father's face that he now suspected the truth. She turned her head and reached a hand out to Noah. He stepped to her side and took her hand in his.

"Dad. Mom. Andrew." She looked at each one of them in turn and then back to her father. "I came back tonight to tell you the rest of the truth and to introduce you to Noah." She looked at Frank and back at her father. "This, however, is not how I meant for you to hear what I have to tell you." Jo pulled her shoulders back and closed her eyes. When she opened them, she inhaled deeply and began again. "Mom. Dad. Andrew. Frank is Tanner's father. Frank is the one who raped me."

Andrew threw his arm around his mother and glared at his father. Peggy leaned into him. Gwen gasped and fell against the back of the sofa.

For a moment, Art sat very still, not saying or doing anything. Then he turned to the man who had been his friend for most of his life and bolted from his wheelchair. "I'll kill you, Frank Richards. I'll kill you!" But before he could take a step, he clutched his chest and fell back into his chair.

"Art!" Gwen reached for her husband.

"Dad!" Jo and Beth raced to his side, Noah one step behind them.

Noah bent over Art. "Jo, call for an ambulance. Beth, if your father has nitroglycerin or baby aspirin, bring them to me."

"He has both."

Beth flew to the kitchen. Jo had already made her call.

Even while struggling to breathe, Art tried to push Noah away.

"Mr. Chandler, I'm Jo's friend, and I'm a doctor. Let me help you until the ambulance gets here. Okay?"

Art nodded once.

Without turning around, Noah said, "Andrew, help me get Mr. Chandler out of his wheelchair and onto the floor. We need to sit him on the floor, up against the sofa, and draw his knees up. Jo, we need a cushion behind his head and one under his knees."

Noah removed the wheelchair's left armrest, and he and Andrew eased Art off the chair and onto the floor in front of the sofa. Jo slipped one cushion behind his head and handed another one to Andrew who slipped it under Art's knees. By then, Beth had returned with the pill bottles.

"Mr. Chandler," said Noah, "I want you to chew and swallow a couple of baby aspirin. Then we're going to put some nitroglycerin under your tongue. And I'm going to be right here with you until the ambulance arrives. I'll ride with you to the hospital. Your wife and daughters will follow us there."

Art nodded and did as he was told. Then he gripped Noah's hand. Within seconds, they all heard the sirens. Jo reached the front door before the ambulance pulled in front of the house. She held it open until the paramedics rushed inside and took over. Then she motioned from the doorway for Andrew to get his parents out of the house.

CHAPTER THIRTEEN

Later at the hospital, Jo and Beth sat on either side of their mother, trying to comfort her. They were having little success.

"Frank Richards has destroyed our family," said Gwen as the tears streamed down her face.

"No, Mom," said Jo. "He has hurt us terribly, but he has not destroyed us."

"What if your father doesn't make it? How can I live without him?"

"Mom," said Beth, "let's wait about crossing that bridge. Let's hope and pray it's decades down the road."

Gwen patted both her girls' hands.

"Mommy!"

Jo looked up to see Paige and Tanner enter the waiting room, both with tears in their eyes.

"I'm sorry, Jo," said Paige. "But when you didn't arrive when he expected you, he sensed something was wrong. He wanted you, and he wouldn't stop crying unless I brought him to you."

Jo took Tanner into her arms. "It's all right, Paige. Tanner, Mommy is here. You can stop crying now."

"Why are you at the hospital? Who is sick?"

"Mr. Art, the man I've been staying with is sick. We're here for him. And guess who's with him?"

"Who?"

"Noah. He's here, and he's with Mr. Art."

Tanner nodded his head. "Then Mr. Art will be okay."

Jo pulled her son closer and rocked him from side to side.

Tanner pulled back and said, "Who are these ladies?"

Gwen and Beth stood and stepped closer. Gwen pointed to herself. "I'm Mr. Art's wife." She turned her head and pointed to Beth. "And this is our daughter Beth. And you must be Jo's son, Tanner."

Tanner nodded. "I am. And I hope someday I'm Noah's son."

Gwen smiled. "You know what? I hope so, too. He's a nice man."

At that moment, Andrew walked into the waiting room, tense and rubbing his hands together.

"Jo, can we talk?"

"Jo," said her mother, "I could hold Tanner while you talk to Andrew if he would allow me to."

"Would you do that for Mommy?"

Tanner whispered, "Is she a nice lady?"

"Yes, sweetheart, she is a nice lady. And Paige is still here. And Mommy is still here. I won't leave this room."

"Okay." Tanner reached his arms out to Gwen, and she welcomed him into her embrace.

Jo joined Andrew in the front corner of the room. "What else is left to talk about?"

"Jo, I died inside tonight. As I got older, I began to suspect my dad was unfaithful to my mom. I even suspected he pursued younger women. I tried to ignore it. I didn't want to believe it, and I never said anything. But I never suspected anything like this." Andrew choked back a sob. "If I had said something back then, he would never have hurt you. We would have married and had a good life together. I'm responsible for all of this. I cannot put into words how sorry I am."

"Andrew, the only thing you are responsible for is not trusting me, and for that I forgive you. You are not responsible for what your father did."

"You tried to protect us all, didn't you?"

"I did. I was eighteen. I didn't know what else to do. Do you know what you and your mom will do now?"

"I know what we plan to do. I hope our plans work out. I wanted Mom to leave Dad and come to live with me, but she said she couldn't do that. Not now. Not with his health the way it is. She said she'd lived with him this long, and she wouldn't leave him now, although she has already moved into the guest bedroom. It seems she'd suspected him, too, but then berated herself for suspecting him. The dutiful wife to the end, I guess. The obedient wife part has ended, though. She put her foot down about what will happen next. She told Dad she could no longer live in that house, and they were going to sell it and move in with my oldest brother. He lives on our grandfather's farm and has been after them to move in with him and his wife ever since Dad's diagnosis. Mom called him when we got home and explained everything briefly, and he said he was still agreeable to the move. He and his wife don't have any children, so that will not be a problem."

"Your dad agreed to all of that?"

"Not at first. He said it would be like being in a prison. But when Mom told him we'd have him declared incompetent if he didn't, and I reminded him prison was where he should be and could end up, he reluctantly agreed. We'll start the paperwork on selling the house and move them to the farm tomorrow. We'll move their belongings as quickly as we can after that."

"What about his health? His diagnosis?"

"He has cirrhosis of the liver. Probably a result of his indulgence in a fatty diet over the years combined with his secret drinking. He dismisses it and says the doctor doesn't know what he's talking about because he feels fine except for a little fatigue. He's not eating like he's used to, though, and I don't think he feels all that fine, but he does a good job of hiding that, too."

"I did wonder about his spider veins. But I haven't been around him long enough to notice anything else. I'm sorry for your family. This doesn't make it any easier, does it?"

"No, it doesn't. Jo, I'm glad Mom overheard your conversation with him. She told me everything. I'm glad we know the truth. You can also rest assured Dad will resign his positions in the church, and we will see to it that he has no access to anyone under the age of eighteen. He will be supervised at all times. He knows the consequences if he refuses. Which brings me to another topic. Tanner."

"What about Tanner?"

"Jo, he may not be the child we wanted to have, but he is my half-brother. How can I not be a part of his life?"

"Andrew, I…. I will consent to letting him know you as my good friend from high school, but that will have to be enough. Can you accept that?"

"I don't want to, but I will. Thank you for that. What about your dad? Do you know anything yet?"

"No, and the longer we have to wait, the more concerned I get."

"Where's Noah?"

"He's with Dad. Otherwise, I would be climbing the walls. Mom and Beth, too."

Paige stepped up. "Jo, I see Noah coming down the hall."

Gwen handed Tanner to Paige, and she, Jo, and Beth met Noah at the door.

Noah pulled Jo close and nodded at Beth and Gwen. "He's out of danger."

The three women shouted and sobbed all at once as they embraced him and each other.

When they pulled apart, Jo wrapped her arms around Noah. "I'm glad you were here."

"Me, too."

"Did he have a heart attack? Is there any major damage?"

"They will keep him at least overnight to be sure, but we all think it was stress cardiomyopathy. Brought on, of course, by the stress and the anger of the moment. He will need to take care of himself regardless. As to that and a couple of other things, he gave me four messages. One for all three of you. Three for you, Jo. The group message is that he will follow all his doctor's orders without question from this day forward, and he will do his best to be a better patient."

"Thank goodness for that," said Gwen and they all laughed. "Now what were the messages for Jo alone, or are we not allowed to hear them?"

"I think it will be okay for you to hear them," said Noah. He took both Jo's hands in his and said, "First, he said to tell you he has some apologizing to do himself. I assume you know what that means."

"I do."

"Second, he wants to meet his grandson as soon as possible."

"That can be arranged."

"Third, he said to tell you that he thinks I am a good man to have around, and he thinks you should seriously consider marrying me as soon as possible."

"Yay!" said Tanner as he slithered out of Paige's arms, ran to Noah, and jumped up into his arms. "Will you, Mommy? Will you? If you do, Noah will be my daddy! Please? Will you?"

"Well, Tanner, I don't think Noah actually asked me to marry him."

"Yes, Josephine Chandler, I did. I am." Noah dropped down to one knee with Tanner on his other knee. "Will you be my wife for now and forever?"

Without a moment's hesitation, Jo knelt in front of them and answered, "Yes, Noah Benson, I will be your wife for now and forever!"

Noah stood and brought Jo into his and Tanner's embrace. He glanced over her shoulder to see Andrew standing there watching them. Andrew's lip trembled, but he nodded at Noah and gave him a thumbs up. Noah nodded in return.

After a moment, Tanner pulled back and said, "Hey, wait a minute. Why did Mr. Art want Noah and Mommy to marry?"

Jo looked at her mother. Gwen smiled and said, "Go ahead. Tell him."

"Because, Tanner Chandler, soon to be Tanner Benson, Mr. Art and Mrs. Gwen are my mom and dad. And that makes them your grandparents."

"I have a grandma and a grandpa?"

"You do."

"Wow!" Tanner held up his fingers and counted them off one at a time. "Tanner. Mommy. Daddy. Grandma. Grandpa. We were two, and now we are five!"

"Make that six," said Jo. Tanner scrunched his eyes. "That lady who was sitting beside Grandma?" Tanner nodded. "She's my sister, and that makes her your Auntie Beth."

"Wow! Now I have two aunties." He grinned and bumped fists with Beth. Then he frowned and looked at Andrew. "But who is he?"

Jo held out a hand for Andrew to come forward. "Andrew is my very good friend from high school, and he would like to be your friend, too."

Tanner smiled. "I'd like that, too." He held out his hand and shook Andrew's hand. "Just one person missing, Mommy."

"Who's that?"

"My Grandpa! When do I get to see him?"

"As soon as the nurses and doctors will allow us into his room."

To that, Tanner answered, "My new daddy can take care of that," and his new family burst into laughter.

After the nurses shushed them, Noah did indeed arrange for Gwen, Tanner, Jo, and Beth to accompany him to Art's room.

The ICU nurse stepped in after them and said, "For no more than five minutes, Dr. Benton, please."

"That's all I need," said Art as he held out his arms to his first grandchild.

Noah sat Tanner beside him on the bed and said, "Be gentle."

"We will," said Tanner as he patted Art's cheeks. "Hello, Grandpa. My name is Tanner."

"I'm pleased to meet you, Tanner." Art brushed away tears and wrapped his free arm around his grandson. "I'm very pleased to meet you."

As Jo watched her son and her father together, she leaned into Noah. She had faced her past, and now, whatever lay ahead, she knew she could face the future and even look forward to it.

AUTHOR BIO

Sylvia A. Nash lives in West Tennessee. She holds a B.A. in Liberal Arts with a major in English and a minor in philosophy. In another life, she taught high school English. Now she spends part of her time wrestling the stories in her head onto paper and part of her time chasing down the stories of her ancestors. To learn more about the author or her books, visit her website at http://sylviaanash.com.

AUTHOR'S NOTE

I hope you enjoyed reading *Facing the Past*. If you did, I would appreciate a short review on the site where you purchased or read this book. I would also appreciate a recommendation to your friends. All writers depend on the recommendations of their readers. I write for you, and I appreciate your comments.

BOOKS BY SYLVIA A. NASH

ENID GILCHRIST MYSTERY SERIES
BENJAMIN'S GHOSTS
MAMA'S SECRET
MARTHA'S GIFT
WILLIAM'S CRY

MILLICENT ANDERSON MYSTERY SERIES
THE MISSING CALICO
THE BOOK OF SECRETS
THE MISSING MANUSCRIPT

STANDALONE MYSTERIES AND THRILLERS
RX FOR RETRIBUTION

WOMEN'S FICTION
FACING THE PAST

SHORT STORY COLLECTIONS
CHOICES AND CONSEQUENCES
BEYOND THE MIST
BIG SISTERS WITH LITTLE SISTER WOES AND WONDERS

VERSE
MEMORIES, A BOOK OF VERSE